BLINDSIGHT

BOOK 1

Susan Peterson Wisnewski

Visit my website at www.spwwrites.com

First Edition: March 2015
10 9 8 7 6 5 4 3 2 1
ISBN-13: 978-1508918240
ISBN-10: 1508918244

Original and modified cover art by Gabor Dvornik and
CoverDesignStudio.com

To Ray, thank you.

CHAPTER 1

L ife can change in a flash without warning and there isn't a thing you can do about it. My life had been an unrelenting rollercoaster ride. One minute I was living the high life with a great job and a stunning Manhattan apartment. In the next, I was living in a musty garage apartment next to my father's house and working for my uncle in Queens. I had become a commuter. No more city girl, no more Manhattan perks. I was shunned to the burbs. The only good thing about my commute into Queens was the Glen Head train stop. When I caught my usual train at eight, the most magnificent creature I'd ever set my eyes on appeared. I called him Sven, the beautiful Norse God of my current fantasies, but I wasn't on that 8 am train, I was heading into work early for a 7 am meeting. Since the train line near my new home is the least popular with the most stops, my only option for today was taking the 5:20 train.

It was destined to be a long boring ride with nothing to amuse myself because I left my phone in its charger next to my bed while in a frenzy not to miss that early train. I wish I could read on the train, but I tend to get motion sickness. Dry heaving is not a good way to start the day. As the train approached the Glen Head station, I did a double take. Sven was standing on the platform looking especially dapper in a dark grey suit. Why was he taking an earlier train? Was my luck changing?

The train was empty. I thought about slinking down in my seat to hide from view, get off at the next stop and reenter at the same stop through the doors at the back of the car. I could start a conversation and well, who knows where that could lead? Thinking about my plan, I figured it would only work if he headed upstairs on this double decker train. My mood elevated. The train stopped and the doors opened. Sven entered the car in all of his magnificence. I let out a short-lived sigh of adoration being careful not to let him see me by hunching down. And then, without warning, behind my magnificent hunk strolled something that could only be described as a Ms. Sven. A gorgeous, tall, blond-haired, blue-eyed, too beautiful to be a model woman was with him. Oh, the inhumanity of it.

My life blows. The pair moved toward the upper level stairs then changed their direction and sat down a few rows behind me, further thrusting the knife that jabbed at my heart. Nothing seemed to be working in my life. It figured the amazing Sven was taken. I went back to my voyeurism since I was phoneless. Funny how I could text and read twitter, but if I tried to read a book I started retching. The sun was beginning to peak out and the darkness was lifting revealing the gray of this April morning. The train clanged past Mineola Station, rocking back and forth as if it were about to derail. I couldn't get used to the motion or the sound of passing trains rumbling by and the awful noise that erupted between the two. Only ten more stops to go. I watched as the landscape changed from suburban trees and well-spaced homes to urban attached homes lacking landscaping that signaled the move from Nassau County into Queens.

As we meandered the long monotonous trudge through empty backyards and later debris strewn industrial lots, I spied two men standing in the street between the warehouses. They looked similar, decked out in their black leather coats and dark denim jeans. Both were large men, perhaps bodybuilders or maybe wise guys. One striking difference between the two was their hair. Both had long dark hair but one wore his in a neat ponytail while the other's was wild and splaying out in all directions. They were arguing. Hands were flying in the air.

Fingers were pointed at each other. The one with the wild hair drew out what looked like a gun from beneath his coat. Time slowed. A shot was fired. Was I dreaming? This couldn't be real. Was someone filming a movie? My heart was racing. Thoughts scattered. I needed to act. I saw the smoke from the gun. The man with the long ponytail fell back. Blood was oozing from his chest. This was no movie. That man needed help. My help. I had to act. Time to fall apart was later. The train moved on. My view dissolved.

"Holy shit," I screamed.

As if in unison I heard a similar shout from a few aisles behind me. Looking back, I could see it was Sven. He looked as stunned as I felt with his mouth agape and a puzzled expression of trying to swallow the horrible deed we witnessed.

"Did you see that?" we asked each other at the same time.

His lovely Ms. Sven was fast asleep. Her mouth was open and I could swear drool was running out the corner of her mouth. She wasn't as attractive in her sleep.

"What do we do?" I asked.

"I'll call 911, see if you can locate the conductor."

Nodding, I raced down the aisle to the conductor's compartment. I banged on the door. There was no answer. I did something I would never do under ordinary circumstances. I opened the door that connects the rail cars, tiptoed over the metal plates saying a prayer that I wouldn't fall through the opening to my death, and jumped into the next car. One of my fears is falling in between the train cars and getting crushed, but extreme circumstances called for extreme measures. I scanned the car for the conductor or another witness, but the two occupants were asleep. I found the conductor booth in this car and as soon as I knocked, the door opened revealing a redheaded, freckled-faced man with a youthful grin whose blue uniform was straining against his girth.

"Did you see what happened?" I screamed.

"Calm down. What happened?" he asked.

"I just saw a man get shot on the street before we got to the Queens border. Did you see anything?

He took a step back into the crowded booth as if he could distance himself from what I was telling him. He wanted the event to go away. He rubbed his hands over his protruding belly letting out a big sigh.

"Oh crap. Are you sure? I was reading the paper. Didn't see anything. Let me call dispatch, this is a first."

He picked up a black walkie-talkie and pressed a few buttons. It made some screeching noises. Talking into the mouthpiece he said, "A passenger just witnessed a shooting, over."

"What? On the train?" a scratchy voice replied.

"No, on the street before we hit Queens," he turned to me, "can you be more specific?"

"It all happened so fast. I was looking out the window and saw two men arguing. The next thing I knew, one of them pulled out a gun and shot the other. It was over in a flash and we were moving at a good clip. I think it was by that fence company. Armstrong or Armada is the name or something with an A. Do you know where I mean?"

"Did you get that? I think she is referring to Armstice Fencing," the conductor said.

"I'll put a call into 911," dispatch replied.

"Another passenger just called 911. He saw it too," I said.

"Okay, conductor, please alert the operator to hold the train. Passenger go to the other witness and see if you can find out if the police will be meeting the train at the next station. I'll call 911 to see what else they might need from us while you get to the other passenger and find out what everyone knows," the dispatcher barked.

I walked back to the car I had been riding in. I wondered, with all of the walking the conductor must put in a day, how he could be so out of shape. It must be a dull job asking for tickets, stamping them and getting asked the same questions day in and day out. He must hole up in his booth and pig out on snacks or maybe when he got home he raided the fridge to overcome boredom. My mind wandered. I didn't want to think about what I had witnessed.

I made it back to Sven just as he placed his phone into his jacket's breast pocket. He was standing in the aisle running his hand through golden locks. Having only seen him from a distance, I was surprised at his height. I'm just shy of six feet and I had to look up to meet his gaze. His perfection factor soared.

"What did the police say?" I asked.

"They want us to talk to detectives and fill out a report. A police car will meet us at the next station. They'll drive us back to scene of the crime."

The conductor's walkie-talkie crackle broke my trance announcing his arrival.

"A police cruiser will pick you up at the next stop. By chance did your friend see the incident?" the conductor asked motioning to Ms. Sven.

Sven motioned to his girl and said, "My sister slept through it."

The smile that spread across my face must have looked ridiculous, but I couldn't help myself. The conductor looked at me as if I were mad. That gorgeous woman was Sven's sister not his girlfriend. Maybe I had a chance. And maybe my bad luck was about to change.

The train stopped at Bellerose Station. The conductor announced a minor delay while the doors remained closed. I wanted to start a conversation with Sven, but what would I say? Hey, did you see the way that guy's chest blew open when he got shot? Or perhaps I could start with, what a way to start your morning, murder before breakfast? Not good conversation. I remanded silent. Finally, two young uniformed officers approached the train and tapped on the door.

The conductor opened the doors and signaled us to follow him. Sven's sister joined us.

"Morning, what's going on?" the taller of the two officers asked.

"At approximately 5:52 am, a Caucasian male, mid 30's, approached same. It appeared there was an altercation. The man who initiated the shouting pulled out a weapon, more than likely a Beretta, and shot the second man in the chest point blank. From that point on, the train took me out of view and I called the incident in," Sven replied.

My jaw dropped. He was smart and gorgeous.

"So are you law enforcement?" the police officer asked.

"Studying to be a lawyer," he answered.

Yeah, it is going to be my day. Handsome, tall, smart and a lawyer; he was a catch. What more could a girl ask for?

"Ma'am what did you see?"

What the hell is a ma'am? I'm twenty-five not forty. People tell me I look young for my age and am forever getting ID'd when I go out to clubs. Ma'am is an over forty dowdy woman. I was dressed casually in dark jeans, black suede booties, a Free People long sweater with a contrasting tank and colorful infinity scarf that was quite chic.

"The same as him. It was at the Armstice Fence warehouse just before we got to the Bellerose Station. The men were arguing. One of them pulled out a gun and shot the other. I got to the conductor as soon as I could, but with the train moving I didn't get much more than they both had long dark hair, had big mustaches and were both wearing dark jeans and black leather coats."

"Okay, we're going to take you to the scene and wait for the detectives. You can give them your official statements."

With that the officers led us down to the cruiser. I scooted into the backseat followed by Ms. Sven and then Sven. We raced through the streets making turns until we descended on the scene of the crime. Police cars, ambulances and policemen swarmed the area. Yellow tape was strung blocking off the end of the street. One of the officers told us to remain in the car. It was impossible to do anything but wait since there were no door handles. My stomach did flip-flops. A sickening feeling enveloped me when I thought about what I was about to see. I didn't want to view the aftermath of the shooting. I hoped the dead guy's eyes were closed. I couldn't bear the thought of looking into dead eyes.

The three of us sat waiting while an awkward silence engulfed us. I could hear my heart pounding and sweat began to accumulate under my arms. I needed to break the silence.

"I'm Tisha," I said.

"Ken, and this is my sister Barbara," Ken offered me his hand.

I looked at his hand that taunted me to touch it. As much as I wanted to shake, I couldn't. I have a secret. I see things. When I touch another person's hand I can see their past, their future, their secrets, and it scares the hell out of me. Two people know about it. Maybe three and I want to keep it that way.

"Nice to meet you. I don't want to be rude, but I'm getting over a nasty cold and don't want to spread it. Forgive me if I don't shake your hand," I added.

I thought about what he said. Ken and Barbara, Ken and Barbie. Well at least we have something in common. We both have parents with a sick sense of humor. My name is, or I should say was, Morticia Adams. My brother was named Gomez William Adams. My mother thought it was cute to name us after strange sitcom characters from the 70s, or so that is what I've been told. She skipped out on my family a long, long time ago. I legally changed my name to Tisha when I turned eighteen. My brother goes by the name Bill, his middle name.

I wanted to make conversation, but didn't know what to say. The thought of what I had just witnessed was weighing me down. The way the victim flew back after he was shot and the blood that spewed from his chest was sure to give me nightmares. The gravity of life and death and it all being over in a second had hit me hard. What could be so bad that you needed to take another life? It didn't make any sense.

An old, dented black car pulled up. The door flew open and an older burly man with a sour expression etched onto his face emerged. His ill-fitting brown suit strained against his weight. The police officer that drove us to the scene opened the car door. I heard the burly man I assumed was a detective bark out, "What's the deal here? Where the fuck is the body? Did you move it?"

One of the officers responded, "We're waiting for forensics. There is no body, but we found blood as well as what appears to be splatter on the car over there." He pointed toward a red Toyota.

Detective Cranky waddled his girth over to the car and yelled out, "Set a perimeter. We don't need any more contamination." He looked over to Ken, Barbara and me saying, "Are these the witnesses?"

Another officer answered, "Yup."

"Come over here," he said pointing to an area away from the blood stained scene.

"You first," he motioned to Ken, "Name."

"Ken Gallant."

"Okay Ken, what did you see?" The detective and Ken walked away so we couldn't hear what was said between them.

Barbara sent visual darts my way and cut the awkward silence with, "It's my first day at my new job and you and Ken had to ruin it with a shooting." She rolled her eyes adding, "There isn't even a body. This is so inconvenient."

What I bitch, I thought, and was proud I kept it to myself. That is another of my shortfalls. I tend to say out loud what I'm thinking and it gets me into trouble.

"But someone might be hurt or dead. Your brother and I both saw the man get shot," I said determined to keep my patience.

"Yeah, but then where is the dead guy?" She reached into her purse and pulled out a mirror. Examining herself, she adjusted her hair and applied a fresh coat of a fruity smelling lip-gloss.

"Good point. I guess whoever did this took the body with them."

"That seems pretty lame. Why would someone want a dead body?"

"Whatever," I answered. Barbara might be beautiful, but I could see empathy and reasoning factors were lacking.

Detective Nasty called me over, "Who are you and what did you see?"

I scrambled over to him feeling like I had been called in front of class to recite a verse I hadn't studied the night before. The only difference was this man had a gun hanging from his side and the potential to shoot if I said the wrong thing. I needed to get a grip. Police didn't shoot witnesses or did they?

"Tisha Adams. I was looking out the window and I saw two men arguing. It was pretty heated. They were chest-to-chest and screaming. One backed up and shot the other. It was like it was in slow motion. I saw the smoke from the gun. The guy who got shot flew back and blood surged from his chest. It was horrible."

"Details, what did the men look like?"

"They both looked similar. Stocky, dark, long hair, tallish, the shooter's hair was wild while the guy that got shot had his in a ponytail, both had large mustaches."

"Anything else?"

I tried to think hard. I closed my eyes and let the scene play back in my mind. "The only other thing I remember was an SUV parked on the side of the street. It's not there now. It was big and black. Maybe it was a Cadillac. I forget what the model name is. Maybe Escalade? Other than that the train was cranking by and we passed where it happened in a flash. I ran for the conductor."

"Okay, I need your contact info." He wrote down my address and phone numbers.

"Now what?" I asked.

"Now we find out what happened. Forensics will come in and see about the evidence and we'll try to trace it. Hopefully, we'll find the victim or a body. We'll do a local search and check the area for any more witnesses."

"If I can help let me know."

"Yeah right. Detective Murphy will drive you back to the train station. If you have anything else you can call him," he said. He stomped away dismissing me.

Detective Murphy walked over to the three of us and led us to his car. He wore dark sunglasses and dark clothes. He didn't say anything, just motioned for us to get into his car. As we drove back to the station in silence, I looked down at my watch. It was seven fifteen and I was fifteen minutes late. My uncle and employer asked me to come in early for a meeting, hence the early morning train. He was going to be pissed. I asked Detective Murphy if he had a phone I could use. Ken handed me his. I dialed my uncle. He picked up on the third ring sounding half asleep.

"Morticia, what's up?"

"Sorry I'm late. I ran into a situation on the way to work this morning. I should get there in about twenty minutes." Even though the job was a dead end, I didn't want to disappoint my uncle. He did offer to help me when I needed him.

"Didn't you get my message? The meeting was changed to this afternoon. I guess you can start early. What happened? Are you okay?"

"I'll fill you in later."

It figured, all this drama and I could have been home sleeping. We arrived at the train station. Detective Murphy raised his sunglasses revealing a handsome face and the bluest eyes I had ever seen. He handed me his business card.

"Sometimes Detective Nelson doesn't have the best manners. If you remember anything else, please give me a call." He winked and lowered his glasses.

"Thanks. I do have one question. If you two are partners, why don't you drive in the same car?" I asked noticing he didn't give Ken a card.

"Long story. Maybe I can fill you in sometime."

"Okay, bye." I wanted to say more but was tongue-tied. Two handsome men in one day was overload.

We made it up to the platform and waited for the next train. Commuters were starting to arrive and the normal morning bustle began. Not wanting to let my opportunity pass I tried to start a conversation with Ken.

"So do you think they'll find the body?" I sounded like a dork.

"I have confidence. Strange though, how there's no body. It's a regular *who done it.*"

"That's what I was thinking. Did you ever study how to find evidence in law school?"

"No, but I did do an internship at a PI firm a couple of summers ago. The investigation team will probably start with a DNA sample and run it for potential perps. If that comes up blank they'll look at missing persons. If that's still a no go, it'll probably go cold. The first forty-eight hours are the most critical."

"What do you think happened?" I asked.

"Not sure. I would say the dispute was over one of two things, money or a woman. The viciousness of the exchange seems to tip to one of those. It is intriguing."

"Yeah," was all I could manage to say. When he spoke his eyes took on a determined glow. I wanted to reach up and throw my arms around his neck, plant a long lingering kiss on those full, pink lips and then run my fingers through the magnificent head of luscious golden locks, but that was fantasyland. If I did that he'd think I was a lunatic.

He reached into his pocket and pulled out a business card. "Here's my card if you'd like to talk more about it."

I did all I could to not swoon. Barbara looked at me as if she were about to vomit.

"The train is here and it's my first day. I can't be late," she said dragging Ken into the train car.

I waved after him cursing the train. It didn't stop in Woodside, so I had to wait for the next one.

"I'll talk to you soon," I called out after him.

The doors closed taking my beautiful Sven/Ken away, but I had a renewed faith in myself.

CHAPTER 2

My job is nothing to write home about. Uncle Chet is my father's brother. He's strange. I'm not sure what business he's in. The sign on the outside of the two-story walkup says insurance and loans, but I don't think that's the kind of business being transacted. I'm the receptionist. I sit in a reception area. It's closed off to anyone entering the office suite with a bullet-proof window and a steel-plated door. I buzz people into the waiting area, they get patted down by one of the large scary men that work for my uncle and then these scary men either give me a thumbs up or down signaling that they can be buzzed into my uncle's office or that they'll be tossed out. A handful of people come in on any given day. My uncle tells me that this is the slow season and things will pick up in the fall. I spend my day surfing the web, virtual shopping and looking for a job. The pay is awful, but some money is better than no money. Sometimes I feel like I'm in a fish bowl. Not an orb shaped bowl, but one of those built into a wall like at some Chinese restaurants. People look into it and I stare back at them. I can't hear what they're saying and have no idea why they're here.

The furnishings inside my uncle's office don't make any sense to me. There are a bunch of desks, all have at least one phone on them, and a wall is covered with TV screens but the volume isn't turned up on any of them. How can he get any work done by watching TV all day and how many calls can you answer at once? I've only gone into his office once or twice. My domain is limited to the front of the suite. The building itself is a non-descript century old walkup you'd find in any neighborhood in Queens or Brooklyn. It's situated on the second floor over retail shops. The store directly below is a nail salon. Whenever I go in to get my nails done they ask me to come back later. Men stream into the store. Maybe it's a men's nail salon or maybe something unsavory is going on down there. The store next to the nail place is a travel agency, and after that there's the deli. They make the best soup around. At least I have that going for me.

The rest of my life is a mess. My dream job is gone. My gorgeous NYC apartment is gone. I have bills up the wazoo and I suffer living in a damp musty detached garage apartment next to my father's house. My new stepmother has cats. I'm allergic to those evil creatures, so no old bedroom for me. Instead I have a couple of zero gravity chairs for a living room, a counter top with a rickety old bar stool for a table and chair set, and my bed. At least I had the foresight to buy a brand new Sealy Posturpedic before my credit went down the toilet. Closet space is a screened off portion of the bedroom. There is a huge mural my brother and I painted on one wall that brightens up the place with its vividness. One summer day when we were bored during a rainy stretch, we found a bunch of paint and created a Jackson Pollack/Monet landscape. It won't win any awards, but I love the colors and it reminds me of the times when we were young and carefree. My brother promised to stop by soon so that he can help me add a fresh coat of paint to the remaining bland white but greying walls. At least the bathroom is decent with a great big soaking tub.

Still sounds crazy? Let me elaborate. Two months ago, I was employed at what I thought was my dream job. After months of interviews and rejection letters, I landed a position with Carlo Mondi, the designer, as his assistant. I didn't read the job description. It was not working as an assistant in helping him with designs, but the job of a gopher. I'd go for coffee, go for lunch, go to the dry cleaner, go for dinner ... you get it. I was a glorified errand girl.

It would have worked if I learned how to keep my mouth shut. Discretion has always been a problem for me. Sometimes I say what's in my head not realizing that I'm vocalizing it. Do you know how it is when you see someone wearing an appalling outfit and you say in your head, "What an awful outfit?" I tend to say it out loud and that gets me into trouble. About a month or so ago, Carlo and I were on a photo shoot. He was dressing one of the models and became annoyed that the drape wasn't to his liking. He kept poking and prodding the poor woman. He backed up from the model to take another look, but as he did his butt came close to my face. I was sitting down on a low stool so I wouldn't interfere with his lighting. That's when I saw it. He was wearing a blue thong under his linen slacks. It looked uncomfortable. Thinking I was talking to myself, I said, "How could underwear up your ass be comfortable, and where do your balls fit into a thong?" I didn't say it to myself.

Carlo, whose real name is Chuck Lefkowitz, had a fit. He prided himself on his appearance. His slacks were draped to flow with his movements, his shirts were starched, bleached and a crisp white with the sleeves rolled to perfection and the shoes always expensive custom Italian with a colorful sock. His face turned from shades of red to blue when he heard my comment. He raised his hand as if to strike me. The weeks of humiliating demands were too much and my mouth exploded with a slew of words I couldn't take back. I don't remember the precise tirade. The general gist was something about him being a fraud and tyrant. I was not only fired, but he made it clear that I wouldn't "ever work in this industry again."

It gets worse. I decided to drown my sorrows at happy hour. I dragged my pathetic soul across town dodging the throngs of humanity headed toward the subway. I entered a shabby watering hole down the street from my apartment and thought my luck was changing as a sign on the door advertised it was lady's night with two for one drinks. I'm not a drinker, but my day was such a bad one I figured what harm could a few drinks do? I didn't have anywhere to go the next day so if I had a hangover, I'd be able to nurse it. I started with a margarita. Then another. I switched to an apple martini followed by a shot of some God-awful creation the bartender was doling out. Before I knew it, I was dancing on a chair ready to jump on to the bar to continue my fantastic moves when a bouncer grabbed my arm and threw me out of the dump.

Somehow I made it the few streets to the apartment I shared with one of my college roommates, Ashley. Making it into the bathroom, I threw up. I gargled, washed my face and headed for my bedroom. I must have made a left instead of turning right. I was drunker than I thought. A few hours later, the lights came on and the screaming began. Ashley was inches from my face calling me a whore. I tried to raise my head, but the pounding from my skull coupled with the shrieks from my roommate were too much. Garnering as much strength as I could, I pulled myself up and asked, "What's the matter?"

"How could you?" she cried.

Ashley was hyperventilating. Tears streamed down her beet red face. I looked over and I saw why she was so upset. Turns out I was in bed with her boyfriend. That jolted me up. I looked over and sleaze ball Trevor was lying next to me naked. Jumping out of the bed, I tried to explain. Showing her I was fully clothed, still had my shoes on, and my purse was slung over my shoulder didn't work. I pleaded with her to hear my side of the story and came close to telling her why I wouldn't sleep with him, but the words wouldn't form. I couldn't tell her my secret.

Thinking about the incident later, I guessed in my inebriated state I must have walked into the wrong room. The apartment was a stunner. It was in Trump Towers, on the forty-second floor. We had views of Central Park, a fantastic outdoor space, and best of all, our own bedrooms. An interior design team was hired to do the decorating. Walking in every night I felt like a princess. Our bedrooms were next door to one another and identical. My room was on the right while Ashley's was to the left. Ashley's father is the CEO of a major investment banking firm. He had paid for the apartment with the condition that Ashley had a roommate. I was the lucky roommate. We split the cable and phone bills. It had been perfect.

Trevor, Ashley's slimy boyfriend, had been trying to get me out of the picture for months so that he could move into the apartment. Ashley and I agreed the apartment would be just for girls. Boyfriends could stay over, but we would let each other know beforehand so as to not create an uncomfortable situation. Ashley had it bad for Trevor. He hadn't given her a second glance until he found out who her father was and where we lived. He was an aspiring stockbroker without a job. He showed up at a party we hosted. Ashley threw herself at him. I tried to reason with her telling her he was a gold digger, but she wouldn't listen. She wanted him and she got him. He tried his best to get me out of the picture. He succeeded.

What a day: a lost job, a lost friend, lost an apartment and got the worst hangover of my life. Things weren't going as I planned.

Finding an affordable apartment in New York City was like juggling elephants—it was nearly impossible. I had no job, my prospects for getting back into the fashion industry were dim and I had over fifty thousand dollars in credit card debt. Did I mention that I'm a shopaholic?

I had no choice. It was back home to live with dear old dad. Don't get me wrong. I love my father and we get along great. There's just one problem—his new wife.

Returning home after being out on my own since college was not an easy adjustment, especially since my dad went out, found and married a strange woman. Her roots are Southern and her speech difficult to understand at best. She wasn't at all the type of woman I thought my father would be attracted to. Beatrice was short, chubby and had close-cropped raven black hair. She also loved cats. I have nothing against cats. They don't like me. They stare, hiss and stalk—and it scares me. It's almost as if they know about my weak spot. I'm also allergic to them. Moving back into the room I grew up in wasn't an option.

My family's home is a beautiful compound in the bucolic town of Locust Valley on the North Shore of Long Island. It is a bedroom community of well-kept large lots and some estates in lush garden settings. It has a wonderful school district and low taxes. It's for old married people not a twenty-five year old woman looking to make it out in the world. It is boring with little to do after eight pm. Even Starbucks is miles away in Glen Cove and I didn't have a car.

I managed to shuffle around my huge credit card bills until my father found out about them. I guess after you move and don't leave a forwarding address or phone number and your bills aren't being paid on time, the companies start calling your references. I liked pretty things that cost a lot of money, but without an income stream things get dicey. No more shopping sprees for me. Dad paid the cards off and now I pay him. My life sucks.

One positive note; my current living arrangement affords me close proximity to the train station. If I hurry down our long tree-lined driveway, scuttle my butt through a side gate and race to the north side of the platform, I can make it to the tracks in less than two minutes. It's literally a stone's throw away.

Since the incident with Ashley all of my friends have deserted me. How could any of them think that I would have anything to do with Trevor? Ashley will figure it out and come around. I just hope it's sooner so she understands Trevor is using her, much better for her than later.

I made a pact with myself to learn about my telepathic ability and use it to propel me forward. My true love was art. Creating sculptures was my calling, but I couldn't figure out how to make a living doing it. Perhaps this hiatus in the burbs would help me rediscover myself.

CHAPTER 3

I woke with a start. I was sweating and my heart beat as if I had just run a marathon. The nightmare that had haunted me as a child was back. The fear of the dark and the demons taunting me were back...in spite of the therapy. I bolted up, but saw nothing. I must be going blind. I shut my eyes and tried opening them again. There wasn't anything but a black nothingness like the disconnected hole my life had become.

I pulled my hand from beneath my covers and brought it to my face but couldn't make out my five digits or the sparkle of the custom made Esmeralda Designs[1] ring my father had given me for graduation. I glanced toward my nightstand, but the alarm clock didn't greet me with its tall, bright, neon numbers and its faint hum was silent. I shifted my gaze to the left and looked toward the window on the far side of the bedroom where the lights that illuminated the driveway should have been shining into my apartment, but the windows weren't visible.

I had never felt so alone. It was one thing to be living by myself, but here I was lying in bed afraid to get up, afraid the darkness wasn't just a power outage with a new moon hampering any possible ray of light.

The realization hit me hard. I was evil.

---

[1] https://www.etsy.com/shop/esmeraldadesigns?ref=l2-shopheader-name

The gift, as my absent mother called it, had come to take me and would lead me into the hell fire world that she had chosen over me. I couldn't let it take me. The darkness had to end. I needed to find the light.

I heard the creaking sound of someone or something climbing the steps to my apartment. A flash of light beamed through the curtain covering the window on the door. I let out a shriek. I pulled my flowered duvet cover closer to my body with the hope it could protect me, afraid to move. A patter against the door erased the silence and a voice called, "Honey are you okay? I thought I heard a scream."

Relief exuded from my pores, "Oh Daddy," I squealed and raced to the door to unlock the latch. "What happened? It's completely black outside."

"Must be downed power lines or a blown transformer. I don't understand why the backup generators didn't kick in. I heard a scream and was worried. Are you okay?" he asked.

"It was so dark. I thought I was losing my mind."

"Honey, you're fine. Everything will be fine." He leaned over and gave me a big hug. I could smell his scent: an earthy mix of musk and sandalwood. He was into incense.

"I brought you a lantern. Should be good until I can get hold of your brother and figure out how he set up the generator. I thought I was the mad scientist in the family able to handle anything, but his configuration has me scratching my head. Want to come down to the garage and help?"

"If you need me, but I don't want to get in the way."

"Honey, don't be silly. I might need an extra hand."

"Okay let me throw on some shoes." I moved the lantern toward my closet and pulled out a pair of sneakers. I sleep in a cozy pair of college sweats and had on a pair of socks.

We walked down the steps to the rear of the garage entering through an already open door. The garage doors were electric and weren't working. As we entered, the hum of a generator started and I could see the lanterns that surrounded our estate blink on casting a warm glow on the property as the garage doors opened.

"I guess everything worked itself out." My father walked toward the far side of the garage to a massive collaboration of machines. He pressed a few levers and punched in a code and everything seemed to his liking. I loved watching my dad work. His intentness was inspiring. He was a biogenetic engineer at a research facility a few towns over. He won lots of prizes for his research and was in demand as a speaker. He was tall, with boyish good looks, surfer dude hair with little signs of grey and a warm smile always plastered on his face. He followed his dream to be a scientist and earned distinction as one of the best in his field of genetics. My brother followed in his footsteps as a scientist, but chose the inanimate rather than the living. He was known as Bot Boy—the robot genius.

Grade school was torture for both of us, as neither of us seemed to fit in. I was a tall, skinny, buck-toothed girl with a loud mouth and strong opinions. Gomez, now known as Bill, was a short, chubby boy with the roundest cheeks imaginable. When we were in middle school he thinned out, shot up and lost the unfortunate Pugsley nickname. He was brilliant when it came to robotics, creating a wide array of inanimate creatures that often chased me around the house and yard in their early formations. He looked like my father. A younger version with darker hair and a slightly sinister demeanor. He wasn't mean, but I wouldn't want to challenge him. He won a full scholarship to Carnegie Mellon and finished his PhD in record time. He was working outside of Pittsburgh for a company developing something he couldn't tell me about. He made a ton of money.

I remained tall and skinny. Thanks to braces I no longer had buckteeth, but instead, as my dentist called it, a toothsome smile.

The wall phone rang, a computer screen lit up and we heard a voice call out, "Hey Dad, Tisha, is that you? Attractive hair. Awake much?"

"Funny. I was scared to death. Between the thunder storm, the blackness in that dungeon and Dad scaring the crap out of me; I think I look pretty good," I said smoothing my hair.

My father gave me a quizzed look.

"Sorry Dad. I'm not used to the apartment. It needs a little more sprucing up."

"You can always have your old room back."

"I'm good. It'll be fine."

"What's going on Bill? Do we have a short in the generator? Shouldn't it have kicked on when we lost power?" Dad asked.

"Not sure. I was in the middle of finishing up my project and didn't get the alert until a few minutes ago. There must have been a surge when a transformer burst. I'm scanning the system now."

"How is your project going?" Dad asked.

"Close to complete, under budget and in record time. If all goes well, I got me a new Tesla. My boss and I had a little wager."

My mouth dropped. I was living above a garage, working for my crazy Uncle Chet, barely scrimping on near minimum wage, and my younger brother would be driving around in a new Tesla.

"I'm happy for you," I managed to muster.

"Since I don't have any reason to have two cars, you can have mine," he offered.

"Oh, Bill, that would be great," I answered attempting to sound pleased. Now don't get me wrong, I was appreciative. Transportation would help me in my pathetic situation, but his car, oh God, his car was a Smart car. I wasn't sure if I'd fit into it. I guess if he could find a place for his head and legs, I could do the same. Thoughts of looking like a clown when I drove about town and got in and out of that car wandered into my head. I'm just shy of six feet tall in stocking feet. Add heels and well, you get the picture. At least I'd be able to get my Starbucks fix.

"I don't know what to say. How can I repay you?"

"Tisha, it's okay. Find whatever it is that will make you happy like Dad and I did." He moved from the screen, some chirping noises in the background took over for the sound of his voice. "Gotta go, my results are in. Your systems should be working. I'll keep an eye on everything. I'll be home over the weekend. I asked to take delivery of the car on the Island. See you Saturday."

"See you then," Dad and I said in unison.

"Well, I'm bushed, a few more hours of sleep then off to start another day," Dad said.

"Night Dad, and thanks for everything," I said leaning in to kiss his cheek.

"Tisha, don't worry, you'll figure out what your calling is and you'll excel at it. Give things a chance. Why don't you take some art classes or how about applying for your MFA? I'll be happy to pay."

"I'll think about it."

He gave me a hug and headed toward the house. I looked around the garage. It was filled with all types of computers, monitors and pieces of robots. Three generators stood in a line humming. There was a workbench with tools arranged in pegs along the backsplash. Mad scientist territory. Maybe Dad was right. There was a calling out there for me. It certainly wasn't in here. As I made my way back up to my apartment, I looked over to my old art studio shed. I hadn't been inside since before college. Maybe I'd get back to my art.

As long as I can remember, I've always been different. Growing up without a mother wasn't easy. My dad did the best he could and my grandmother, my dad's mom we called Grams, came to live with us helping Dad raise us. I hated whenever we had anything to do in school that required a parent. Dad was always there, but a snide remark or look from a classmate was inevitable. No one knew what happened to our mother. Us kids included.

There was also the other thing about me that made me different. I learned to keep it to myself at an early age. Not only can I read a person's hand, but I see things. Shadowy figures of people or sometimes animals appear and then *zap* they're gone. From the time when I was about five, one of them would come to me in our rose garden. She said she was a fairy. Her name was Boon. We would wander through the garden plucking the largest most vibrant rose and then dance in delight as we placed it in the stone fountain watching the beautiful flower float.

I made the mistake of telling one of my schoolmates about my fairy friend. Instead of keeping it a secret like I asked, she told all of the other girls that I was a baby and made up imaginary friends because I had none of my own. It took months of teasing before my classmates went on to torment another child. That solidified my resolve to keep my mouth shut about my abilities.

My brother believed I could see things. He wasn't able, but had faith in me just the same. When I asked Grams about this cute creature, she became upset and said I'd turn out just like my mother. I had no idea what that meant as no one ever talked about her. I pretended my mother was dead. It was easier to think she was gone rather than that she left my family by choice. As I got older I stopped wondering about my mother and didn't go out to the rose garden at dusk. When you don't get real answers you stop looking.

CHAPTER 4

A week passed since the shooting. The dead body still hadn't shown up, but even more disturbing was a man that looked like the victim had been following me. He would appear out of nowhere and then *poof* he'd be gone. I can't recall ever having the same spirit, I guess is what you'd call it, come to me other than my fairy friend. It was time I found out what the hell was going on. I tried calling Detective Nelson, but he didn't return my calls. I'd left messages for Detective Murphy, but no return calls from him either. I called Sven, I mean Ken, but he hadn't heard anything new and I wasn't sure if it was too soon to call him again.

Searching the web for answers was like spitting into the ocean; too much stuff not enough of what I need. I needed to find out more about my gift/curse and was determined to find answers. There was a shop in Sea Cliff that sells all kinds of spiritual stuff. They had tons of books, perform readings and have been around for a long time. I figured maybe they could lead me in the right direction. Perhaps if I could channel this man that's been following me, I would be able to find out who he is and what happened to him. Plus, I'd be able to come to grips with my abilities.

Work was quiet. It was just my uncle, a burly door guy and me without much to do. Burly Door Guy was sitting down in one of the black plastic chairs with his eyes closed. I bet he was asleep and snoring. His wide chest rose up and fell down in big waves. He must be bored out of his mind too. I wondered what he thought about when there was nothing happening. At least I could play games on the computer, shop and web surf. As I contemplated the virtues of salad over soup for lunch, it happened. The door opened and a man walked in. Burly scuttled to his feet so he could maul the visitor. At first I didn't get a good look, but as Burly patted the stranger down he turned toward me.

"Holy shit, it's him," I shrieked to myself. Before me stood the wild haired, mustached man that shot the other guy. What could I do? Do I tell my uncle? What are the chances that he would just show up here? What if he found out there were witnesses and he was here to kill me? I had to warn my uncle. I buzzed him holding my hand over my mouth so Mr. Possible Killer couldn't lip-read what I was about to say.

"What's up sweetheart," Uncle Chester asked.

"Uncle Chet, the man who's here to see you, there's something about him I think you should know."

"Brickyard Mike? What about him?"

"I think it's him. I think he might be the killer."

"The killer of who? I know he's a hot head, but a killer, come on."

"No, listen. He looks like the guy I saw shoot the other guy on the train last week."

"Tisha, come on now. That was a long time ago. You saw this guy for what maybe ten seconds and the train was moving. Mike's a standup guy. He wouldn't shoot anybody."

"I'm worried about you." I was pacing back and forth in my cubicle.

"Don't be. He's here for a pick up."

"What do you mean?"

"Don't worry about it. You can buzz him in when Igor is finished checking him."

"If you say so. Be careful."

He laughed, "Careful isn't in my vocabulary."

I placed the phone back into its cradle. I didn't know what to do. My stomach was in knots. My head was pounding. My flight or fight response was activated. I had to do something. Finally, a lead in the case walked right into the office, slapped me in the face, and yet I had no idea what to do with it. I pulled out my cell phone, not wanting to leave any computer trail at the office and googled Brickyard Mike. Nothing. I opened a file drawer. Dust wafted from it due to lack of use. I scanned the B's, the M's and then went through all of the files trying to find something with information on this man. Again, it was a dead end. I had to find out who this guy was and what his involvement with the murder might be. I had to be sure that he wasn't the murderer or if he was, he needed to face the music and be brought to justice.

I texted Ken, *I think the perp is in my office.*

Nothing.

I texted Detective Murphy the same message as I sent to Ken.

What do you mean? the detective texted me back.

A guy that looks like the perp walked into my office. His name is Brickyard Mike.

Is Brickyard his first name?

Not sure.

I was kidding. Why is he in your office?

Client of my uncle.

Ok. Let me see if I can find anything. Are you safe?

Behind bulletproof window.

Where do you work? A bank?

No, insurance agency.

Are you sure?

Well...

Did you call 911?

Not sure if it is him so no.

What time do you get off?

This was getting interesting. *Four, you?*

Same. Want to catch up and compare notes?

K. Where?

There's a pub by Mineola Station, the Davenport. On your way home?

Sounds great, see you then.

I texted Ken to let him know what was happening, hopefully, he'd be able to make it too.

Brickyard Mike finished whatever he was doing with my uncle and walked out of the office. As he strolled to the exit door he looked over his shoulder and smiled at me. It sent chills down my spine. There was no longer any doubt in my mind. It was him.

Call me a worrier. I buzzed my uncle, "Everything okay?"

"Yeah, he made me a little lighter, but that's okay."

"What do you mean?"

"Don't worry your pretty little head. Listen; tomorrow I was hoping you could do me a favor. I need to drop some papers off in the city, but I have back to backs all morning. Would you mind taking care of it for me?"

"Sure. Where and when?"

"That a girl. Come in regular time, I'll have the package ready and let you know where to go. Listen, it's quiet, I'm heading out. Why don't you call it a day too?"

He didn't have to ask me twice.

"Have a good night Chet. See you in the morning," I said.

I had about two hours before I was meeting Detective Murphy and hopefully Ken. Even though I was broke, that didn't stop me from shopping or at least looking. Foxes, a designer discount haven in Mineola, was next to the Davenport and two hours left plenty of browsing time. Maybe my life was turning around and the suck factor was ebbing.

I walked the couple of streets toward the train platform. Spring was beginning to make its appearance. A few trees were beginning to bud and the sun felt warm on my face. The winter blahs would soon be over. The short walk relaxed me. Out of nowhere, the peace I was enjoying came to a halt and a gnawing feeling in my gut kicked in. It felt as if I were being watched. I turned around a few times, but didn't see a soul. I climbed up the stairs to the train platform. It was empty save a few construction workers on the other side of the tracks traveling into Manhattan. Their train came first. They got in and I was alone.

I sat on a bench and pulled out my phone to find when the next train would arrive.

"Can you help me?" a voice asked.

I looked up. It was the dead guy. I grabbed my purse pulling it toward me as if it were a shield. I muttered, "Who are you?"

"He has to be stopped."

"I can't help you until I know who you are. What's your name?"

His mouth tried to form a word, but then as he was about to utter something a noise from the staircase startled him and he vanished. A few teens in Catholic school attire joined me on the platform.

This went from crazy to insane. Not only did I see dead people, now they talked to me. I needed help big time.

CHAPTER 5

I made it to Mineola Station without additional spirit visitors. I was still shaking. I knew I needed help. Apparitions were one thing, but now these beings were talking to me. It made me think of Mom. My mother left when I was a young child. I don't remember her. A picture of her with Bill and I sat on the mantel in the living room until my dad married his current wife. I never knew why she left, but I did learn that she was some sort of witch or seer. Her mother, my grandmother Fiona, visited from time to time, but my dad was less than cordial during her short visits. I'm not sure exactly what transpired between them. Once I heard them talking. Dad said she reminded him too much of his wife and it upset him to see her. I did know that my father loved my mother and it tore him apart when she left.

I walked through the crowded aisles of Foxes without seeing anything I was interested in buying or trying on. The vision left me distracted. I didn't want to be anything like my mother, but I knew that wasn't the case. Maybe if I found out what happened and why she left I could come to terms with the gaping hole in my heart and make some sense of my own strange abilities that were spiraling into high gear. Maybe this was all meant to show me who I was and what I could do with the gift. Or maybe it was another dead end. There was one way to find out. I needed to call Fiona.

I checked my phone. It was almost four. I left the shrine of deep discount designer clothes purchaseless and made my way to the Davenport. The restaurant had a wonderful scent of fresh baked bread mixed with garlic studded roasting meat. My mouth watered. Making my way to the bar, I found Detective Murphy seated waiting on his drink.

"Hey, detective, what's shaking?"

"Hi Tisha. Glad you could make it. Call me Murph. Can I get you a drink?" He stood up as I approached, pulling out a barstool and helped me sit.

"Sure. How about a Pimm's cup?"

"Good choice. I just ordered the same. I love the way the cucumber and lime mixes with the herbed gin. So refreshing."

Murph was dressed in a pair of jeans, a blue oxford button down and a navy sport jacket. I hadn't notice the sparkle in his eye, the perfect shape of his face or the strong chin with just a small scar when we first met. He was hot. As I leaned in to get a better look, the door opened and in walked the magnificent Sven/Ken.

"Oh look, Ken's here. I figured I'd invite him too so we could all put our heads together on this and see what we come up with," I said.

I noted a sign of unhappiness on Murphy's face. He rose and shook Ken's hand.

"Good to see you. I'll get the first round. What'll it be?"

"Bud," Ken answered.

Not a very exciting choice of beverage. Ken's allure was dimming. At least he could have gone with one of the forty or so craft brew selections. Maybe he was thirsty.

The drinks arrived and we sipped.

I started, "I know it sounds strange, but here goes. I have a photographic memory. This morning at work a man came into my office and I think it was the killer. The only reason I'm a little hesitant to call Detective Nelson is because he scares me to death. I don't want to be wrong and get an innocent man in trouble."

"But if you have a photographic memory, how could it be wrong?" Ken asked.

"We were a distance away from the crime scene and it all happened so fast. I would say I'm eighty percent certain."

"Were you able to find out his name?" Murph asked.

"Just the Brickyard Mike thing. I didn't want to worry my uncle. He put me off and said he was a standup guy and wouldn't have anything to do with killing anyone. I'm going to snoop around the office more tomorrow. Maybe I'll come up with something. My uncle doesn't have the best filing system."

"Anything you can get on him would help, like where he lives or works. Without a body and little evidence, I'm holding off on questioning this Brickyard guy," Murph added.

"I'll give it a try."

"I'll do a lexis/nexis search," Ken said.

"Okay, but unless he's already in the system, it won't shed much light. I'll ask around in the neighborhood. I'm new to this detail so I haven't gotten my feet wet learning the locals. My partner knows everyone both on the Nassau and Queens sides. He's laid back since he'll be retiring in a couple of months. I'm sure if there's a story to go with this guy, he'll know about it."

As Murph was talking, I was distracted by Ken's constant motion. He couldn't sit still for a moment; fixing his hair, straightening his slacks, checking his phone, crossing and uncrossing his legs. It was like watching a five-year-old that was asked to sit still. It was starting to get annoying. Before I could say anything Murph said, "Dude, what's up? Didn't take your Ritalin?"

"Sorry, sitting on the train and then in the office all day gets to me. I haven't worked out in almost a week. I gotta get to the gym."

"I hear you, brother. Okay, how about we start asking around and see what we come up with. We can compare notes in a few days."

"Sounds good," Ken answered. "The train to Glen Head will be here in two minutes, Tricia, want to join me?"

"It's Tisha, sure."

Then, I knew for sure. Murph was not happy. His smile turned to a scowl and it looked as if he were a moment away from striking Ken. Could it be he was interested in me?

"Okay a few days, but if anything happens before then, I'll give you call."

I patted Murph on his solid shoulder and made my way to the train platform with Ken. The train arrived as scheduled and we boarded. The car was crowded so we stood in the vestibule.

"So where do you work out?" I asked, tucking my hair behind my ear.

"At home mostly. I have a setup in the garage. I also try to make time for the facility that's in my office building, but I wind up talking shop with coworkers and can't concentrate on my reps. I like the solitude of working out alone."

"Do you think we're going to be able to find out who this guy is?"

"Of course. It would be great to wrap this all up one, two, three. It would get me far."

"What do you mean?"

"Oh, well nothing. It would make me happy that justice was served."

"Oh, okay. Me too."

Ken was confusing me. I thought he was a lawyer. Something wasn't adding up. I couldn't think of another thing to say. Ken seemed so shallow or maybe he was boring. Could be he was shy. No one that looked as good as he did could possibly be boring. I figured I'd try another angle.

"So where do you go after work? Any fun spots in the city?"

"I usually go home and workout. This past week's been a bear with so much going on." He was staring out the window not looking at me.

"Any hobbies?" My desperation had to be showing.

"I like to run, oh and bike ride."

"I love bike riding. There's this great path in Locust Valley that winds around past Beaver Dam and then down to the beaches in Bayville. Have you ever gone that way?"

"No. Been to Bayville but not a Dam."

"Well, this weekend's weather prediction is supposed to be warm and sunny. Want to join me?" I blurted.

I did it. I asked him out. Butterflies were swarming in my gut. I thanked God I was wearing layers so the sweat that began to exude from my armpits and back and was dripping down the crack of my ass wasn't visible. What was he going to say? Was I doomed to be living a celibate, loveless life in the burbs or was there a hint of chance, a possible connection?

"Let me check my schedule."

He opened his phone and started typing. The horror I felt, the gnawing in the pit of my stomach, the shear panic of possible rejection made me come close to vomiting. And then his mouth began uttering the words that would either elate or deflate me. I watched as if in slow motion as his perfect mouth formed the following words.

"I guess I can make it as long as it's around eleven."

"Great it's a date. I'll meet you at the Locust Valley train station at eleven and we can go from there."

"Okay, but don't be late. I'm always on time."

"Me too," I called after him as he descended the train and was off to his home in Glen Head.

Thinking about his answer, and the way he was borderline rude, I came to the conclusion that he was just awkward. With those looks he had to have one flaw.

CHAPTER 6

F riday had always been my favorite day. The thoughts of a fun weekend were looming in my mind and the possibilities of fun put me into a happy, carefree mood. I had a date. Maybe not a go out to dinner or club date, but a bike ride could lead to an all-day into the night thing. Doing my usual commute and stop at the deli for coffee, I hummed my way up to the office. I put the key into the latch and went about my daily routine of turning on the lights, backing up the computer server and turning on my computer. Candy Crush was eagerly awaiting my arrival until Uncle Chet showed up. I played the game and won three new levels in minutes. If that were any indication of my day, it was destined to be a good one.

Uncle Chet waved as he came into the suite and disappeared into his office carrying his coffee with a newspaper shoved under his arm. In a minute he buzzed me.

"Still game to go into the city for me?" he asked.

"Sure," I answered.

"Okay, I'll get the parcel ready. Be out in a few minutes."

I turned back to my computer and continued the inane time waster. I needed to think about a better way to spend my time. Perhaps I'd try an online course or maybe learn how to do complex animations. Something, anything, would be better than stomping out pieces of odorless, tasteless fake candy bits.

Uncle Chet knocked on the window to my fishbowl and I buzzed him in. His hand shook when he placed the package on my desk. He took the shacking hand in the other and massaged it.

"Damn arthritis is killing me," he said.

"Would you like me to get you some aspirin?" I asked.

"No. I'll be okay. Sucks getting old. Anyway, I need you to bring this to an office building on 36th and 10th. Here's the address. Ask for Richard C," he said handing me one of his business cards with an address scrawled in his slanted writing.

"Will he be giving me something in exchange?" I asked.

"No. He said to head over at about eleven. Might as well call it a day after that. I know I haven't been giving you much work to do, but I'm happy you're here. The busy season is coming up, so it will be hectic then."

"It's fine Uncle Chet. I'm happy you gave me an opportunity when I needed one."

"Your dad and I don't see eye to eye on much, but I'm glad I could do something for the family."

He reached into his pocket and pulled out a hundred dollar bill.

"Have a little shopping spree on me."

A huge smile spread across my face. "Uncle Chet, I couldn't," I said taking the bill before he could return it to his pocket.

Letting out a little laugh he said, "That's my girl. You're more like me than you know."

I had no idea what he meant, but a hundred bucks is a hundred bucks. He kissed me on the forehead and made his way back to his office shutting his door. The gorilla of the day arrived and I waved to him. Two more hours to go and then off to the city for an errand and then down to Century Twenty One for a little weekend date wear shopping.

The hours flew by and I was off. I made my way down to the train depot and headed into the city on the 7 subway. The hustle and bustle of people moving about, jockeying for seats on the crowded car, all mixed with the anticipation of a fun weekend was intoxicating. The subway car made its way over the 59th Street Bridge and down into the labyrinth of the bowels of New York City. The creation of such an elaborate system of railways all interconnected and transporting millions of people around the greatest city in the world on a daily basis with little calamity was one of those things that gave me hope. I was no dummy. A little distracted, somewhat confused and lacking real direction, but if someone could dream up and create this elaborate maze that enriched the lives of so many, I could figure out a way to get my act together and make my contribution in the world. I believed my world was about to change and head into a new exciting direction. I was ready.

I hopped off the train at Times Square Station. The lights, neon signs and Disneyesque atmosphere greeted me and matched my mood. Hurrying along Broadway, I made my way over to 39th Street, then to 10th Avenue and finally over to 36th. The streets were empty before lunch. After lunch was another story. I searched for an address on the prewar buildings, finding a small gold and white marble placard with the address my uncle gave me. I pressed a gold doorbell and waited for a response. Nothing. I pressed again. Still nothing. I pulled out my cellphone and called my uncle. The call went to voicemail. I left a message and then texted him to find out what to do. I noticed a café across the street. With an entire day ahead of me, and cash in my pocket, I went inside. Sitting at the counter I felt like I was taken back in time. There was a large mirror on the back wall pitted with age, juice fountains swirling neon colored concoctions, the counter was a thick massive wood gleaming with a coat of wax surrounded by a brass rail to rest one's feet on. I ordered a coffee waiting to hear back from my uncle. As I waited, I flipped through my purse and came across Ken's business card. The address revealed his office at a mere street away from where I sat. As I pondered the significance of my discovery, my phone beeped indicating a text. Peering down, my uncle assured me his client was in the office and to try my drop off once again. I collected my bag and made my way to the building. This time, as I rang the bell the door buzzed open. I entered a shabby entryway and was facing three doors. Not knowing what to do, I did nothing; standing, waiting for an indication of where to go. A few minutes passed and one of the doors opened. A short, wiry man appeared.

"You from Adams?" he asked.

"Yes," I answered.

"Got the package?" His eyes darted about the small room.

I reached into my bag and pulled out the bundle.

"Here you go," I said handing him the bag.

He took it, opened it and peered inside. Closing the bag he backed up into his door placing his hand behind him to turn the handle and disappeared back into his office. Something wasn't right. That little voice in the back of your head that gives you a warning signal was screaming. I pulled my bag in closer and made my way back out onto the street. I didn't want to know what was in that bag or what my uncle was involved in. I needed a job and the extra cash he laid on me was welcome, but I decided his drop offs were too sketchy for me. Next time, I would think twice about a delivery.

Taking a few breaths, I decided to pop in on Ken. Perhaps we could have lunch or coffee. I wasn't sure if he would mind, but what was the worst that could happen? Say that he was busy? I could live with that.

His office building was one of the new high-rise buildings that were sprouting up all over the west side. The area, once the garment district, was dubbed West Chelsea. The sleek lobby was designed in natural wood varnished to a shine with exotic plants dotted about adding to the airy vibe. I walked over to the building directory, found his floor and made my way to the bank of elevators. I pressed the up button and stepped onto the elevator car that opened before I had a chance to chicken out and run from the building. The car propelled me up its tube ascending to the twenty-ninth floor. Doors opened and I read the sign and followed arrows to my destination. I turned the corner and was greeted with a wall of glass doors. A vast reception area sported several comfortable looking couches, a parson coffee table between them with magazines strategically placed upon it. Three people manned a long marble counter. There were two young women and a man. I did a double take. Ken was seated at the counter donning a headset. I was confused. I snuck back around the corner to get out of his view. I pulled out the business card he gave me from my wallet. It had his name, all of the information for the firm, but no title. Was he a receptionist? His allurement factor plummeted again.

I headed back to the elevator, but before I pressed the down button, I decided to think about this situation. Maybe he was an intern and had to man the phones today. Just because he was seated at the counter didn't necessarily mean anything. I had been wrong before, so I did an about face and made my way back to the office. As I entered, Ken looked up. Meeting my gaze, he held up his finger signaling me to give him a minute. He completed his call, removed his headpiece and came around the counter to greet me.

"Tricia, what a surprise. What are you doing here?"

"It's Tisha. I had an errand to run for my uncle a street away and I thought I'd stop in and see if you'd like to have lunch," I said giving him my best smile.

"My break isn't until 2:30 plus I have errands to run. We're meeting tomorrow."

"Oh, well, like I said, I was in the area. By the way what do you do here?" The question fell out of my mouth.

"Right now, I'm the telecommunications coordinator. I have a few more courses to complete and then onto studying for the bar." As he spoke his eyes darted about, he swayed from one foot to the other and he kept picking at his shirt. "I gotta get back to work. See you tomorrow." He raced back to his station, placed the headset on and went about his duties.

Too much about this day wasn't adding up. First, the strange delivery to my uncle's client and now the bizarre reaction to me from Ken had me scratching my head. Instead of a trip downtown and shopping, I decided to call it a day. A long hot soak in my great big tub would wash away the creepy feelings.

CHAPTER 7

Saturday arrived. I woke at seven with nervous energy. I couldn't sit still and since Ken and my plans were to go for a bike ride, working out wasn't a good option. I busied myself cleaning my apartment. I dusted, vacuumed and rearranged my paltry furnishings. Then a thought came into my head, what if the ride went well and he wanted to stop back in? I searched through a dresser drawer and found some candles and a vase. I checked the fridge. I had two bottles of Starbucks Lattes and a shriveled apple. Not good. I threw a jacket on over my sweats and headed toward the market. It was only a few streets away, but boy did my neighbors look at me like I had three heads as they passed in their cars. Walking was not the preferred method of transport in this neighborhood. Unless you had a dog tethered to you or were clothed in exercise gear, walkers were met with suspicion.

Once in the market I headed down the aisles and placed some fresh fruit, sparkling water, cheese, crackers and a decadent looking chocolate raspberry cake in my basket. In front of the checkouts, I spied a pretty flower arrangement and added it to my purchase. I considered stopping at the liquor store, but wine or champagne at eleven was pushing it.

I strolled back to the house getting even more questionable glances. A few neighbors even stopped to see if my car broke down and I needed a ride. Honestly, suburbia was not for me.

I placed my purchases in the fridge, arranged the flowers in a vase and decided to take a hot shower. It was heaven. After moisturizing my skin, it was time to choose what I would wear. I ravaged through my workout gear and found a new pairs of leggings and a yoga top I don't remember purchasing with tags still attached. I added a nylon jacket, running shoes and my bike helmet. It was quarter to eleven. Rather than pace, I decided to head over to the station. I could always do a few laps around the block until he arrived. As I crossed over the tracks, I could see he was waiting at the station building. I waved, as I got closer.

"Hi Ken, you're early."

"Wasn't sure how long it would take for me to get here from home. I don't like being late. Where too?"

"I figure we can ride down Buckram Road, take a left at Lower Horseshoe, then over to Beaver Dam. We can stop there for a breather, and then take it up over the hill and down Bayville Avenue to Stehli Beach. It's a really pretty stretch of Long Island Sound."

"Okay. You start. I'll follow," he said.

I began cycling only to find him giving me directions from the rear. If I heard speed up, watch the driver, are you sure you know where you're going, or can you move a little faster once more, I was going to turn around and clock him. He turned from man of my dreams into an insensitive, narcissistic asshole. But maybe he was just nervous. I'd wait until the ride was over to see how he acted.

It didn't get any better. We made our way back to the station and he told me he had to go because he had another engagement and rode off. Nothing else. I was wasting my time. He was a loser. The "date" was over in forty-five minutes.

I stopped at the local deli so I could drown my pitiful bad date by indulging in a greasy egg, bacon and cheese sandwich, but the line was so long I headed back home. My brother's car was parked in the driveway. I hadn't seen him in weeks and needed some cheering up. I knocked on the front door and went inside. I didn't feel comfortable strolling in. I didn't like my father's new wife, Beatrice, and I had no idea how she felt about me. They had been married less than a year, but I knew next to nothing about her. I had about four minutes before the cat dander would assault my nasal passages resulting in a sneezing, coughing fit, so I looked down at my watch and began the countdown for the visit.

"Bill," I called out, "are you home?"

"In the kitchen," he answered.

I walked down the long hallway and toward the kitchen. Beatrice hadn't done much in the way of redecorating the house save their bedroom and I was glad. It felt good to have the stability of my childhood home in my life even if it was in four-minute increments. The kitchen was a semi-circle with a wall of windows overlooking the patio and gardens outside. A hint of color was beginning to emerge from the grey shades that settled in for winter. Various bulbs were waking from their slumber and in a few short weeks the garden would take on an opulent display of vibrant color. I poured myself a cup of coffee and asked if anyone needed a warm up. Bill lifted his cup while Dad declined.

"So when does the car get here?" I asked.

"Any minute. I feel like a kid at Christmas," Bill answered rubbing his hand together.

"So what did you do to get a Tesla?" I sat down with the guys at the table.

"Saved them money," Bill replied with a sly grin.

"Must have been a ton. Those go for what? Like over a hundred grand?"

"About that. So how was your date?" Bill asked.

"It was a bike ride." Rolling my eyes.

"And? Details, dear sister."

"My four minutes are almost up. Gotta go."

"Not so fast. I'll walk out with you."

My dad shook his head. "I made reservations for dinner tonight at Twin Harbors for seven o'clock. Shall we all go together?"

"We'll meet you there," Bill answered following me out of the house.

"Crappy date huh?" Bill asked.

"Not the worst, but he wound up being a real jerk."

We made our way through the breezeway and climbed the stairs to my apartment.

I slumped down in one of the lounge chairs trying to think of something to say to change the conversation, but I couldn't come up with anything. I had a crappy job, no friends, a pathetic love life and a dead guy was following me. I wanted to bring up the dead guy, but I didn't know where to start. The day belonged to Bill and his achievements not me and my problems.

The silence inside ended when a horn sounded from outside. I'm not sure who jumped up quicker, Bill or me. We raced out the door and down the steps to find a sleek new Tesla gracing the driveway. Bill had the widest grin ever on his face. Dad stepped outside with Beatrice and was beaming. His pride couldn't be contained. One day, I promised myself, he'd look at me like that too.

"I'm so pleased that you've become such a success Bill. All your hard work is paying off."

I think I saw a hint of a tear in Dad's eye.

I gave Bill a hug. "That is one amazing machine."

"Well what are we waiting for? Let's take it for a spin," Bill called out adding,

"This is the p85, their top of the line model. I had a hand in some of the design details. This thing is freaking awesome." We found our seats, sat back and enjoyed the ride. Bill drove the same way as the bike ride I just endured for its beauty and the lack of other vehicles on the road. It was an amazing ride.

Back at the house Beatrice reminded Dad that they had a lunch appointment and scurried him to her car.

Bill turned to me once Dad and Beatrice were out of sight, "Okay, what gives?"

"I've been seeing the dead guy."

"What dead guy?" His eyes popped.

"The one I saw get shot. He's been coming to me trying to communicate."

"When, how? That is fascinating."

"It's random. At first I thought someone was following me, but then Thursday I was leaving work and on the train platform and he appeared. He asked me to help him. Some kids came up to the platform and it must have scared him away. I don't know what to do."

"How about finding out from someone who does know?"

"And how do you propose I do that?" I was beginning to get a headache. I knew who he was referring to, but I was afraid. How could I call Fiona out of the blue and expect her to drop everything and help me? She hadn't made any effort to contact me in years. I thought that maybe after college she might come around, but not a word. I didn't know where I would even find her or if she dropped off the face of the planet like my mother.

"How about we start by trying that shop in Sea Cliff. They might be able to steer you in the right direction. And if all else fails there's always Fiona."

"I thought of going to Sea Cliff. In fact, I was going to go over today. I don't want to involve Fiona."

"Your choice. I'll join you. This is so cool."

I loved my brother. He was an off the charts genius, but still marveled at something that could be explained as my over active imagination. At least I had one person I could count on through anything. I hated not knowing what happened to the man who got shot and on top of getting shot his body was still missing. If I could help this poor soul that needed it, I would.

Growing up without a mom had been tough, but you get used to the way things are and don't look back. Fiona had tried to be part of our lives but Dad pushed her away. I needed Fiona, but was terrified that she would turn her back on me if I reached out to her. My ability to hold onto people was not good. Maybe it was a defense mechanism, not making connections with people so that I couldn't get hurt if the other person didn't feel the same way about me as I did them. It happened with friends, boyfriends, and now the possibility of with family. Maybe, if I learned more about my gift, I could overcome this relationship phobia.

We drove down Forest Avenue through Glen Cove and then over to Sea Cliff. Bill drove to the end of Sea Cliff Avenue and found a parking spot that afforded him extra space and the possible chance of another car not getting too close. We crossed the narrow street and walked into the Victorian house that sported signs with times for workshops, psychic readings and their hours. The scent wafting through the door was a mixture of assorted incense and luscious candles. Mobiles and chimes hung from the ceiling greeting us with their lyrical sounds. The shop was crowded with a number of people waiting for a workshop to begin. I went to the back of the shop that housed bookcases overflowing with all sorts of metaphysical books. Bill went into the adjoining room that was filled with loads of paraphernalia and well-worn sofas. As I scanned the book titles, I felt a hand tap my shoulder.

"Hi Tisha," a vaguely familiar voice called out.

I turned and saw her. It had been years since our last visit. She hadn't aged. Her platinum hair was long and flowing, her skin taut, vibrant with a glow and her eyes sparkled a shimmering deep dark blue. Those eyes, the dark blue eyes that peered down at me from the mantle of the marble fireplace in my father's living room, were the eyes I had come to hate for abandoning me, and the eyes that were looking into mine right now. All reason told me it wasn't her. It wasn't my mother, but all the same I felt my mother's presence. I needed to escape. I tried to speak, but the words hung in my throat. All the rehearsals in front of the mirror I practiced should this day ever come vaporized in a flash. I couldn't stand the thought of Fiona and Bill ambushing me. I pulled my purse in tight and ran out the door.

Looking left then right, I didn't know where to run. I decided on right as I could catch the train to Locust Valley from Sea Cliff Station and crawl into bed forgetting this day.

"Wait," Bill called after me.

"You're an ass," I shouted.

"Would you please slow down and wait for me to catch up."

I stopped. Dark clouds were descending and I could smell the whiff of rain coming. Not wanting to get soaked in a downpour, I weighed my options as Bill neared.

"Why did you do that to me? I wasn't ready for that," I said.

"Tisha, Fiona can help. You know it as well as I do. She has the gift and so do you. You're like a super hero," he said grinning like one of the demented waving cat figurines we had encountered.

"But she's part of that woman who left us. I don't want anything to do with her."

"Suit yourself. I was just trying to help."

"Help me by coming back with your car and driving me home. I don't want another chance encounter with the witch."

"Fine, but she does want to help. I think you should give her a chance."

"Maybe, but if I do, it will be on my terms."

Watching Bill walk to the car, I could see Fiona standing on the steps of the shop. Bill stopped and spoke with her and then made his way to his car. She glanced up the street to me and then turned, walking back into the shop.

My brother and I drove back to the house in silence. As he pulled into the driveway, I unlatched the car door and bolted up to my apartment before he came to a complete stop. He didn't follow me. I needed time to think. I had to plan my next move and then I had to apologize to my brother for acting like a child and then to Fiona for being rude. Both would have to wait as the sleep that eluded me the night before came. I made it to my bed and collapsed into the warm duvet and had a dreamless slumber.

CHAPTER 8

Waking from my sleep refreshed, I decided to put my plan of attack into motion. First, I called my brother. It went to voicemail. I hung up. I googled Fiona, but couldn't find any info on her. I guess it served me right. I had to suffer alone.

I decided to do an online search for contacting the dead. I was amused to learn there were over nine million charlatans offering advice for a mere $9.95 per ten minute session. Checking out the book selection on amazon, I was happy to find many authors decided to go the free route with prime borrowing. I spent the afternoon downloading from their library and learning that I don't know the first thing about communicating with the dead nor do most of these people that write about it. I needed help.

My phone buzzed that I received a text. I peered down at the lit up screen.

Happy with yourself?

Bill.

Call me, I texted back.

A few minutes passed and finally ringing.

"I'm sorry," I said.

"About what?" a stranger wondered.

"Oh, I thought it was someone else. Who is this?"

"Murph, the detective. We met a couple of weeks ago. Missing dead body…"

"Oh, hi. What's up? I was expecting a call back from my brother."

I switched the phone to my other ear and walked over to the bathroom mirror and rearranged my sleep-mangled hair.

"Looks like we found a body."

"Oh my God, really? Who is it?" I began pacing.

"They're doing preliminary work right now. He washed up along Jamaica Bay so it's not a good sight, but it appears to be a man reported missing a few days after you witnessed the shooting. The descriptions match. I don't have a name yet."

"Do I need to identify the body?"

"No, he's too far gone for that, but when we get positive confirmation, NYPD will probably show you a photo of him when he was seeing better days. It would help to identify him as the victim in your shooting."

As he was talking, I heard a knock on my door. I pulled back the curtain and saw Bill standing on the landing. I opened it and let him in. I went back to my call.

"So now it goes to the NYPD? I thought because it happened in Nassau it would be a Nassau case."

"The body was discovered in Queens. Until we know that it is our victim, it's in the city's hands."

My brother started tickling me. I kicked him away trying not to laugh.

"Thanks for calling, I gotta go," I said. Before I hung up, I heard a hesitation in Murphy's voice. I clicked the call off before I had a chance to process the possibility that the call wasn't over. I made a mental note to call him later.

"So ungrateful, mean sister what's this with the NYPD? Who was on the phone? Did they find the dead guy?"

"I deserve that. It was the detective on the case. It looks like they found the body. They need to make a positive ID and then they want me to verify that it was the guy I saw get shot."

"That's good. Now you don't need to find out who the dead guy is."

"They think they know who it is. They're waiting on positive identification. Maybe my follower will leave me alone now."

"Maybe. I hate fighting with you. I'm going to say this, even though I know it's something that you don't want to hear. You need to ease up on Fiona. It's not her fault our mother walked out on us. Mom walked out on her, too. She walked out on everyone. Give Fiona some slack and try to get to know her. You might just surprise yourself."

"You're the forgiving one. I'm the mean ungrateful one. It pisses me off that someone could have two kids and walk away from them like they didn't mean anything to her. I've thought of what I'd say to her if she ever came back and it isn't pretty. It's the picture, you know, the one that Dad had on the mantle growing up. Fiona looks like an older version of the picture of Mom. I freaked."

"She does look like our mother. Why don't you try to talk to her? You never know, you may find whatever it is that keeps you from getting what you want will be resolved once you understand your gift better. Doesn't seem like you have an incredibly busy schedule."

"Thanks for reminding me. I tried to find her number but there wasn't anything in the book."

"I'll text it over to you. Be gentle with her. Fiona is an amazing lady and we are all she has."

"Got it. Bill, I am sorry."

"Don't worry about it. Now are you going to get dressed? I have been salivating all day thinking about the shrimp scampi appetizer I'm going to dig into at Twin Harbors."

"Yummy. I hope they have the French Onion soup on the menu. If not I'm going for the Lobster bisque. Be ready in a sec."

I dashed into my bedroom and pulled on a pair of black jeans, a black cotton sweater and a colorful scarf. A quick dab of face powder, blush, mascara and sheer pink lip-gloss made me ready.

"Let's go chow down," I said. As we made our way down the steps to his awaiting car, that gnawing feeling of doom reared its ugly head. Something was going to happen. I didn't know what or when, but I knew it would.

CHAPTER 9

I was getting accustomed to the commute into work. Two months of traveling and I was able to take a nap and wake up just in time to get off the train at the Woodside Station. Work was boring, but I decided to make the best of the time trying to figure out what I wanted to do with my life, so instead of passing time surfing the web every day I began thinking about how I could go back to my art and build a career.

Art classes were forming and I knew that getting back to sculpting was a step in the right direction, plus Dad would pay for the classes. There were so many choices in the online catalog. It was time to pick something and go with it. I was tired of complaining and moping around. How could I ever be happy until I grew up and took control of my life? My cell phone buzzed. Searching through my bag, I pulled it out. There was a message from Murph. Hmm, what could he be calling about at this time of the morning? His shift ended about now; maybe he had news about the victim.

I looked down and read, *DO NOT go into work today.*

I typed back, *why?*

Let u know later, do NOT go in.

On train, almost there.

Have breakfast with me.

I need to call my uncle.

Don't, will explain, meet me in the city.

Where?

Penn, what train r u on?

Let me look, I looked up the schedule and texted, *Hicksville, arrive at Penn, 8:23.*

K see u in a few.

How odd. Why couldn't I go to work and what did my uncle have to do with it? The train arrived at the Woodside Station and I remained seated. That's when I saw him. Brickyard Mike was standing in the middle of the platform looking up and down trying to see who was getting off the train. I slunk down in my seat, but it was too late. He recognized me and headed onto the train. Since it was my usual train and it was rush hour, there were no seats available and people were standing up in the aisle. He stood about ten feet away glaring at me. The conductor did his walk through the train car calling out for tickets. Brickyard was not prepared. He needed to purchase one. As he reached into his pocket for cash and looked away from me, I texted Murph.

Brickyard got on train and is staring me down.

Keep away from him. Is the train crowded?

Yes.

What car are you in?

I don't know, switched at Jamaica, toward the middle.

Is there a number?

Where?

By the doors.

Car 789.

K, calling backup. Stay away for him.

He's the 1?

We'll see.

Losing service going into

Shit, I was cut off before I could send him my last text. Service is spotty at best in the tunnel under the East River. I put on my sunglasses hoping they would somehow shield me from Brickyard. I wondered how he got his name. Was it because he was built like a brick wall? Or did he eat bricks for breakfast? I felt like I was going to throw up. Was he after me? Was he going to try and kill me like he did with the dead guy? Did he really kill the other guy? How did he know I suspected him? The conductor's voice over the loudspeaker cut my thoughts. *Next and last stop Penn Station, please look around and collect your things.* I needed to keep my cool a few minutes more. I hoped that Murph had a team of police with him. Brickyard was looking meaner than ever.

I stood up and made my way for the doors furthest from Brickyard Mike. As an experienced commuter knows, once one person makes their move for the doors, their fellow commuters join in scrambling for position to be the first out the door. I wanted as many people between me and my nemesis as possible. The doors opened and I bolted out. I looked to my left and then to my right, but no Murph. I ran for the stairs, but as I did I felt a hand grab my arm.

A voice whispered in my ear, "Say a fucking word and you're dead. Come with me."

Looking up, Brickyard Mike looked even meaner than I imagined. His teeth were clenched, his eyes steel and I could smell the anger on him. I didn't know what to do, but when I felt a jab in my side with what can be only described as a gun, I acquiesced.

Brickyard led me down the end of the platform to a door. He fumbled with the lock and opened the massive steel door whose latches squealed. He squeezed my arm harder and tried tossing me into the room. I yelped in pain and struggled to free myself. That's when I saw out of the corner of my eye ... Murph was on the platform across from us.

"Police," he screamed, "let her go."

"You going to stop me? You and what army?"

Mike pulled me closer and pulled his weapon from his jacket pocket. It wasn't a gun, but a long thick knife. He brandished it with skill and brought it to my chin.

"Come any closer and I will filet her."

My heart was racing, sweat spewed from every orifice of my body, my head was pounding. I couldn't spend another moment in this monster's clutches. He tipped his knife into my throat. I could feel the blood trickle down my neck and its coopery scent wafted into my nostrils. My flight or fight response kicked in. With every ounce of my might I drove the spike heel of my beloved Jimmy Choo boots into his foot. He reeled back screaming, but not before he sliced my neck with another of his knife techniques. I could feel my skin open. The blood ran out of my wound like a faucet being turned on. The sound of a shot rang out. Brickyard fell to the ground. I could see smoke coming from Murph's gun.

Time slowed as if a pause button was pushed. Brickyard fell away from me clutching his chest. My hand went to my throat, trying to stop the bleeding that started gushing. My mind was at full throttle. I knew I only had seconds. I moved toward the dying man. I reached down and grasped Brickyard Mikes hand. I braced myself for what I would learn. To my horror, I found out the truth. He didn't do it. He didn't kill the dead guy.

BLINDSIGHT

BOOK 2

Susan Peterson Wisnewski

CHAPTER 1

Blinking open my eyes, I thought *where am I?* Was I alive? There was a golden stream of light coming in through a huge picture window. I slowly became aware of feeling in my body. I was in a bed with various tubes jutting out of my arms and an oxygen mask over my face. My head hurt and I couldn't think straight. I had to remember what happened. Everything was fuzzy. Maybe I died and I was in purgatory waiting for my audience with St. Peter. I strained to focus and listen, but there wasn't a sound save the blipping noise the machines connected to me were making. *Why isn't anyone around?*

I tried to think back to where I was before I wound up in this bed. I remembered commuting into work on the railroad. I was almost at my Woodside stop when I got a text message from Murph. He was the detective that I met when I witnessed a shooting. He told me not to go to work. He asked that I meet him for breakfast in the city and he would explain why I should stay away from the office. Something happened after that, but I couldn't remember what it was. On the train there was someone that upset me. The rest was a blank. My head hurt.

Back to the *am I alive question.* If this were purgatory, I don't think I would be strapped to a bed. I wouldn't be in pain or at least I don't think I would be numbed by drugs that are beginning to wear off. Maybe I'm in a hospital. That would mean nurses. I was never really in a hospital before. Other than the one emergency room visit for a fractured wrist when I fell off my bike, I've for sure never been in a hospital room. That's where I must be. I tried to lift my head and see if I could find a phone. Dizzy was an understatement. I took a deep breath and tried again. There was a phone on a tray table. I reached out to slide it closer. I picked up the receiver, but to my horror there was no dial tone. *Now what?*

I was getting agitated. The pain medication was wearing off. My throat ached. My mouth was as arid as the desert and had the taste of a blend of metal and unbrushed teeth. Raising my hand to my throat I felt a bandage running from ear to ear. I fumbled around looking for something to call a nurse with. When I attempted to speak pain stabbed through my neck as if someone were trying to behead me. A flashback jolted through me. That was it! I was stabbed, well not stabbed. Brickyard Mike tried to slit my throat.

I witnessed a shooting a few weeks back and suspected Brickyard Mike was the killer. I had the chance encounter with Brickyard at my uncle's office. I work for my uncle as a receptionist. Murph called and told me not to go into work and would fill me in on why over breakfast. Brickyard came on the train, followed me and then attacked. As he was about to slit my throat, Murph shot and killed him. Before Brickyard died, I reached out and touched his hand. It was then that I knew he wasn't the killer. I have this ability to see people; their past, present and future by touching their hand. After that everything goes blank. I needed to find out where I was and what was happening to me. Then I needed to talk to Murph.

Sitting up was not working. The dizziness was now morphing in comparison to the nausea. It was clear. I was going to barf. I reached around searching for a bucket, a trash can, anything where I could spew my guts. And then I saw it. A buzzer was lying next to me. I clicked and held my mouth closed as best I could trying not to heave my stomach contents.

The door began to open. Rather than relief, I was in a panic until I saw the nurse.

"Hey, you're awake. How are you feeling?" A nurse in green scrubs walked over to the side of my bed.

"Hurt," was all I could manage to mumble. My tension eased; it was someone here to help me not complete the unfinished task of removing my head.

"You have a serious wound, but don't worry. The doctors fixed you all up and you'll be good as new in no time."

"Vomit," I rasped out between clinched teeth.

"Oh boy," the nurse grabbed at the nightstand next to me and pulled a small yellow basin from it. She brought the tub up to my mouth and held back my hair. There wasn't much coming out, more retching than anything else.

"There, there. I'll get the doctor to give you something for the nausea. Don't want those stitches coming out."

"Where is anyone?" I sounded illiterate in my haze.

I couldn't go through this alone. Where was my dad and Bill, my brother, and what about Grams? I needed my family. I'd even take Beatrice, the stepmother I hardly knew. What happened? Did anyone know that Brickyard Mike isn't the killer? There was still a murderer out on the loose. I needed to talk to Murph. I needed a hug.

"Your family was here all night. They went downstairs to get some breakfast. I'm going to give you a little something for the pain. Is that okay?"

I waved my head like a frantic puppy waiting for a treat. In a moment it was lights out. I never had a high tolerance for drugs.

My eyes began to open. This time there was a huge bouquet of the palest pink peonies on the rolling cart next to my bed. Their gentle grace was a beautiful contrast to the bulky stark machines that surrounded me. I remembered an entry from a book on flowers I studied as a child that peonies are the flower of healing. Dad and Bill were sleeping in chairs pulled alongside my bed. The door opened and my grams walked in.

"Get up you two. Our Fairy Princess is awake," Grams said as she walked over to the bed poking the two on her way to me.

Leaning in she gave me a big kiss on the cheek and then nestled beside me placing her arm around me.

"What a scare you gave us all. How are you feeling? The doctor said you'll be fine in a few weeks. I made sure we had the best plastic surgeon take care of that nasty cut. We don't need anything to remind you of that horrible day or to mar that gorgeous body. Another day or two and you'll be back home."

"How are you feeling?" Bill asked.

I managed, "...sore, hurts ta talk."

"Don't worry sweetie. It will all be over soon and you'll get back your voice," Dad added.

"The one time I don't want you to shut up. Figures," Bill said.

I couldn't help but yawn. Every inch of my body ached.

"Get your rest honey. We're not going anywhere," Grams said.

I closed my eyes and drifted back to sleep.

~ ~ ~

In a deep sleep, I was running down a corridor trying to get away from someone. There were other people walking through the pathway. They passed me by, but seemed not to see me. In order to get away from my attacker, I had to dodge these throngs of people. I pleaded with them with my eyes to help me, as I was unable to speak. My pursuer was a man. He was getting closer and closer. I waved my arms, grabbed at the people around me, but no one would help. He was inches from me. Drawing a dagger from his waistband, he held it high overhead. I could hear the swishing sound as it drew down, plunging down and striking me over and over. Blood spewed from my arms, my chest and my neck. I fought with all my strength. I tried to scream. I flailed my arms and darted my eyes to the people that walked past me without giving me a second thought—hoping, praying someone would help me. I kicked and clawed, but was losing strength. I felt a hand on my shoulder.

"Wake up, honey. Wake up."

I opened my eyes startled to see my father leaning over me. I tried to jump up, my head pounding.

"It was only a dream. You're in the hospital. It was a dream. You're safe now. No one is going to hurt you again."

The words assured me for the moment, but I knew the dream would come back. My black nothingness dream that taunted me as a child returned and now it was in Technicolor and upgraded. The evil inside me was attracting more evil. A nurse entered the room, checked my vitals, and after some whispering with my father, emptied a few syringes into my IV. I fell fast asleep. This time my slumber was dreamless.

CHAPTER 2

T he next couple of days were a blur. I was in and out of consciousness. Doctors came and went. My dad, brother and grams were with me whenever I woke. Some friends popped in for a few minutes. In my drugged state, I didn't remember who came, but I did know there was much activity. My father's wife came. I know that because I could tell by the smell of the perfume she wore and the sneezing that ensued from the cat hairs she inadvertently brought with her, but we didn't talk. I thought I saw Murph at one point, but wasn't sure. As day turned to night, I became more lucid.

A doctor examined me, asked me a few questions and reassured me that all was going well. I was on my way to healing and would be released once he consulted with one of the other doctors. I was relived. Hospitals are not fun. They're scary and creepy and it's impossible to get a decent sleep. Every time I was finally getting a good rest, I was woken up, poked, prodded, injected and examined. It would be a welcome change to be home in my musty garage apartment.

The doctor gave word to the nurses that I could be released. Released sounded so ominous. Was I in danger? I wondered what was going on with the investigation. Other than Murphy's visit, there weren't any police officers asking me questions. While having that thought, two men in dark suits entered the room. In my drug-induced state, I couldn't help but recall the movie *Men in Black*.

"Morning Ms. Adams. I see you're ready to be released. I have a few questions for you. Do you have a minute?" the one with the darkest hair asked.

As if on cue, my grams entered the room. She looked from one to the other with a cringe-worthy scowl.

"Identification, please," she demanded.

The officers gave her an unhappy glance and produced their credentials. Grams looked at them and said, "Can't this wait? My granddaughter has been through quite a trauma."

"Time might be of the essence," the blonde one replied.

"I'd like you both to consult with the family attorney first. I would prefer she answer questions after she is released." Grams pulled a business card from her purse handing it to them. "Here's their information. If there isn't anything else, I will see you out."

Grams took each by the arm and came close to throwing the men from the room. My grandmother might appear to be a Locust Valley lockjaw, lady who lunches—the proverbial WASP with her St. John's suits, proper pumps and impeccable coiffured hair—but she was also a powerful businesswoman, plus her mama bear instincts were in overdrive. She walked back into the room closing the door behind her.

"How are you feeling today sweetheart?" she asked.

"Like someone tried to slice my head off," I answered.

"The doctors claim you'll make a full recovery. Before your dad and brother get back, I'd like to ask you a few questions. Really, it's one question. What happened?"

"I've been playing it over and over in my mind. Here's what I remember. I was on my way to work. Murph, he's the detective working on the shooting I witnessed. Well, he texted me that there was a development in the case. He wanted to talk to me about it and asked me to meet him at Penn Station. He was adamant I didn't go into work. As the train pulled into the Woodside Station, Brickyard Mike, he's the guy I thought might be the shooter, was on the platform and came onto the train when he saw me. The next thing I remember was waking up here in the hospital."

"You don't remember the shooting?" she asked.

"What shooting? I was stabbed. Who was shot? Wait you mean Brickyard?" Gram's face showed no sign of wavering. She would ask the questions. I was to answer.

"You said you thought this Brickyard character did it. Why *don't* you think he did now?" Gram's lips were pursed and she was wringing her hands.

"It's coming back to me now. Brickyard got closer and closer on the train, when we made it to Penn he grabbed me and tried throwing me in a storage room. Murph shot him. I reached down and took his hand. I know he didn't do it." My head was pounding. Images of that morning flashed through my mind.

"Honey, Detective Murphy found you just in time. You're safe now." She smoothed my hair adding, "Brickyard Mike has an alibi for the previous shooting. He had an arrest record a mile long. He was involved with something else. It had to do with your uncle. Do you know anything about that?"

"I just sat in the cubicle thing and let people in and out of the office. I don't have a clue about what Uncle Chet does. Is Uncle Chet okay? And what about Murph? He must be torn up."

"The detective will be fine. He seems like a good man. He was very shaken. He's stopped up a few times late last night."

"What about Uncle Chet?"

"Your uncle seems intent on putting me into an early grave. He's in serious trouble. This time I won't bail him out. We're not sure where he is. You need some rest. I'll be back later. We can go into details when you get home." She kissed me on the forehead and walked out of the room. The familiar sound of her heels hitting the ground in a determined fashion gave me comfort. I closed my eyes and fell fast asleep.

When I woke, a nurse helped me dress and then steadied me as I got up and sat in a wheelchair. Bill carted me to the front door of the hospital where we waited for Dad's car to appear. The flash of cameras blinded me starting right when I tottled out of the wheelchair trying to get to the car. My father shielded me while Bill wheeled me right up to the awaiting car. Shouts of questions were thrown at me, they all garbled into nonsense. I didn't understand what was happening. Who were they asking about? The killer who wasn't a killer? I heard Chester Adams a few times. I was astounded at the number of reporters and the questions they were asking that made no sense.

The two scooted me into the backseat of the car and we pulled away from the curb, away from the hospital, and were bound for home. Secured in the car, I turned to Bill, "What's going on?"

"All kinds of stuff." He nodded to the front seat and my father mouthing *later.*

Dad turned around, "Sweetheart you need to heal. I don't want anything else to worry you."

"Okay," I answered but knew there was so much more at stake. I closed my eyes and let the soft sounds of the classical music on the radio relax me. I thought about what had happened to me. It was hard to comprehend that I was nearly killed. I didn't have any idea why. I couldn't understand how such awful people could be in this world. I needed to find out more of what happened. I knew that my father was shielding me, but that was of no help to me. It was time for me to face the music, what happened to the dead guy and my special power.

CHAPTER 3

Having made it home without any further incident, my dad pulled into the driveway and helped me out of the car. This constant handholding was getting on my nerves.

"Dad it's my throat, not my legs."

"Honey, I know. I understand. It's just I was so afraid we were going to lose you. You might be dizzy."

"I'm afraid too. I want all of this to go away."

The three of us walked up the stairs and into my apartment. Before I could turn the doorknob, the door flew open and Beatrice greeted me with a hug.

"So happy you're home. How are you feeling?" she drawled in her thick southern accent.

Walking into the apartment, I couldn't believe my eyes. What was once an awful smelly garage storage space was transformed into a beautiful apartment. My dream board had taken shape, going from flat corkboard pinups to full-fledged life. There was a grey velvet sofa and flowered chairs from Anthropologie, a glass coffee table from Crate and Barrel between them. A wall of bookcases now separated my bedroom area from the living room which was filled with my books, a new flat screen TV and a Bose wireless speaker system. A new mini kitchen gleamed with its wall of high gloss picket fence white cabinets and to my delight was equipped with a Wolfgang Puck pressure oven and Jura espresso machine. My rickety table and chairs were replaced with a round marble table and black lacquered rattan chairs. I took it all in and then, as only I can manage to destroy such moments, said, "What the hell did you do to the walls? Where is the mural?"

I regretted it the second the words erupted from my mouth. Attempting a replay, I said, "I'm so sorry. I didn't mean it like that. I'm still fuzzy from the painkillers. It is beautiful. Thank you."

Beatrice's mouth hung open. She swallowed hard and said, "Well how about you get some rest." She turned on her heel and walked out of the apartment. I could see a tear on her cheek.

I can count on one hand the amount of times I saw my father get angry. I added another to the list. He opened his mouth to speak, turned, shook his head and said, "I didn't think you would mind that Beatrice took the liberty of making your dream a reality. If you want to be angry at someone, make that someone me."

I didn't know what to say or why I blurted out such noxious words when she was simply trying to make me happy. In fact, I liked all that she had done. I said, "I'm so sorry Dad. That's not what I meant to say. I don't know what's wrong with me. I'm overwhelmed. It's a real home now."

"Well, get some rest. I'll check on you later. If you need anything, Bill set up an intercom system next to your bed and beside the couch. He'll show you how to use it." Dad walked out of the room with his shoulders slumped.

"Great job. What are you going to do for an encore?" Bill asked.

"Oh shut up. I've already had my throat slit. How about a knife through my heart?" I asked.

"I think I'd have trouble finding it. Tisha you've got to ease up on people. Stop shutting yourself away. She's his wife and it doesn't look like she's going anywhere other than as far away from you as she can get. At least make an effort."

"You're right. It just came out. Remember that day we made that mural?" I was trying anything to get Bill back in my corner. I sat down on the sofa and pushed one of the gorgeous tapestry pillows under my head.

"Yeah. It was pouring outside for days. Seemed like an eternity to us kids. I swear I thought grams was going to strangle the two of us with our whining and what do we do now questions every three minutes. Good thing she had a bucket full of paint and brushes lying around. We worked on that disaster for two days."

"Disaster? I liked it. Gave the room character," I said.

"It was a train wreck. A demented, childish attempt to cover a wall with crazy paint. This place is beautiful now. Maybe I'll invite Beatrice down to my empty apartment and let her do another amazing job. Oh, but I'll be grateful and thankful."

"Thanks for making me feel even worse. I'll make it up to her," I said.

"Yes you will and sooner rather than later," Bill said sitting down on a chair. He placed his head in his hands, pulled his fingers through his hair and looked at me, "Tisha, I think you're still in danger. We didn't want to say anything while you were in the hospital, but well, here goes. Brickyard Mike and Uncle Chet were involved with some unsavory characters. There was gambling, loansharking, prostitution and maybe even some drugs. The Feds were closing in on the operation and were raiding the office when you were attacked. Uncle Chet disappeared. They think Brickyard Mike was tipped off so he stayed away, but was watching from a distance. When you didn't arrive to the office, he went looking for you. At least that's what the Feds are saying. What do you think?"

I shook my head, "I think I have a headache. I had no idea what was going on in that office. I've told you that. Murph called me and asked that I meet him in the city for breakfast. I was unsure because I didn't want to upset Uncle Chet, but he made it clear not to go into work. I guess he was trying to warn me of the raid."

"You would have been better off working for that crazy designer."

"I should have filed for unemployment when I lost that job. Or better yet, I should learn how to keep my mouth shut. If I did, I'd still have my Trump Tower apartment and a potentially good job."

"Don't forget a stepmother who doesn't hate you," Bill added.

"Thanks for the subtle reminder. I'm going to take a nap and then apologize."

Bill got up and walked over to the intercom on the side table. "This is simple to use. See this button here?" he asked, pointing to a big red button adding, "press it and talk. It goes directly to the house and downstairs to my work area. If you can't press it, yell. It's voice activated for high pitched sound."

I looked from the intercom to him, "Do you think someone is after me? What do you mean your work area downstairs?"

He got up and placed a hand on my shoulder, "Call it intuition, but I don't think this is over. Dad and I had a talk. Until we know what we're dealing with, we're all staying close. I can work from anywhere. Downstairs is as good a place as any. Dad hired a security team to keep an eye on the property. Security at his lab is top notch. He'll be safe. Grams will be staying at her cottage here instead of in the city. Beatrice will curtail her comings and goings or have one of the guards drive her to where she needs to go."

"Seems like you two have it all covered."

"Let's hope so. Now get some rest. If you need me, I'll be downstairs. If I'm not there, I'll be in my old room." He kissed my forehead. "I'm so glad you're okay. I don't know what I would do without you."

"Oh, Bill. You're the best. Love you," I said giving him a big hug. I plodded into my bedroom to find even more of Beatrice's handiwork. My bed was adorned with a stunning canopy, an armoire graced a wall and the nightstand held a lamp shining on a special golden clock I thought I misplaced. Its housing sparkled and its hands keeping perfect time. I owed this woman more than an apology. Diving under the covers, the apology would have to wait until I woke.

CHAPTER 4

Waking from the first restful uninterrupted sleep in days, I heard my phone buzzing. Opening my eyes, I was amazed at the transformation of my space. Once drab and almost utilitarian, it now had a modern, welcoming vibe. I owed Beatrice big time. I found my purse and pulled out my phone. The call was gone. Searching the message button, I learned it was Murph who called. I texted back, *how are you?* Nothing. After about five minutes I got my response.

Been better. R U home?

Yes, glad to b out of hospital.

We need to talk.

Big time, I typed.

What's good for you?

Still on the mend. Tired. Tomorrow?

Time?

Working?

No

10 good?

Where?

My place. I typed in the address.

Later.

I wondered how he was coping with the shooting. He must feel horrible. Life and death and it all being over in a matter of moments and then having a hand in that decision was still too much for me to wrap my head around. I liked pottery and sculpting and making things—much more up my alley than life and death decisions that needed to be made in a spilt second. I didn't know how I was going to live with myself. It was me who caused all of this trouble. My misguided attempt at helping the shooting victim find his killer wound up getting the wrong man killed. It was an honest mistake, but now a man was dead. The guilt enveloped me. The disgust I felt for what I did was almost too great to bear, but then I told myself that things happen for a reason. I needed to find out what that reason was. More, I needed to find out why Brickyard was willing to kill me, and if that was why he was following me on the train.

Before I lost myself in my grief, I decided to at least attempt to make amends with Beatrice. Searching through the cupboards, I found that I was stocked with all kinds of glorious food. I made short order of mixing stirring and combining my ingredients for a batch of my killer brownies. Popping them in my new oven, I set the timer. I stepped outside and looked around. I found exactly what I was looking for. There was one forsythia bush that hid behind the garage and bloomed before the others. I clipped a few branches and secured them with twine. I made my way into the garage and opened a closet I hadn't opened in years. It was the accumulated art pieces I had created over the years. I found an interesting aqua blue vase that was tall and heavy and placed the branches in it. Back up to my apartment, I rummaged around and found a beautiful spool of white velvet ribbon. Art school came in handy at times like these. I skillfully arranged the flowers and tied a bow with the ribbon. The brownies were cooled and I arranged them on a platter. Making my way down to my father's house, I hoped Beatrice wouldn't slam the door in my face. I rang the bell. Nothing. Tried it again, but no answer. I took my sorry gift back to my apartment and called down to Bill.

"Hungry? I made brownies."

"Be there in a minute."

I guess there would be tomorrow to try to ask for forgiveness.

CHAPTER 5

Three days. I had been in the hospital for three days. It seemed like an eternity. I didn't know exactly what Murph wanted to talk about, but had a good idea. At least I didn't have to panic about my pathetic house. And I had food and coffee. He said he wasn't working, I hoped that it was his day off and nothing more. I heard a light knock on the door.

"Come in," I called.

"Hey," Bill said as he pushed open the door.

"Hey yourself, I need a hug."

Bill came and grabbed me in one of his bear hugs. He smelled like soap and a hint of the cologne I gave him as a stocking stuffer for Christmas. My brother was always my rock. Growing up we were the two oddballs in the neighborhood. The kids without a mother and whose father didn't set many boundaries. We were curious and got into fun trouble. We also saw things that no one else did. I had the gift of touch; I would touch a person's hand and be able to see their past, present and future. Bill had the gift of sight. He could identify a problem and see things that would help overcome the problem and then build something to solve it. We debated about the terminology of our gifts. He believed that it was I that had the gift of sight since after touching I could see, while his was a gift of seeing and then innovating so he called it natural insight. Call it semantics, but I believed that my sight was blind because I didn't know what to do with it. He was working at a scientific think tank as well as a robotic company coming up with futuristic designs that were revolutionizing robots and industrial design, all at the ripe old age of twenty-four. Me, I hadn't come up with a way to put my gift to use. I still needed to figure it out and I knew that this was what our conversation would be about. He released me from his hold.

"Nice digs, Beatrice outdid herself."

"She did. She used my dream board and brought all the clippings I had on it to life getting almost everything there in a way that fits into this ... well, it feels like a real apartment now."

"What's missing? I'll get it for you," Bill offered plunking down on a chair.

"Can't, it's the paintings and sculptures I keep promising myself I'll create."

"What are you waiting for? Seems there's a rather large walk-in downstairs full of sculptures and art you did create."

"Bill don't be silly. I need to earn my keep. I can't just sit around making art. That junk downstairs is amateur."

"Why not? That can be your job."

"Who will buy it? Plus it's not that simple," I said.

"Why do you always complicate things? You are talented. You need to believe."

"I believe I owe Dad like fifty grand and I don't have a job. I need to make money."

"We'll figure something out."

"So what's up?"

"Just wanted to check on you. Looks like they rounded up Uncle Chet last night. He is in deep doo doo. Neither Dad nor Grams has been able to see him. Between you in the hospital and him in a federal jail, Grams is ready for a breakdown. She even wore slacks to go into the city with Dad."

"No way. Slacks are weekend only wear. She must be beside herself."

"I always knew Uncle Chet was cut from a different mold, but this is over the top. Reporters have been calling the house. There's even a small contingent of paparazzi outside the gates. Adams family tragedy must sell newspapers. The cops are going to be questioning you about Uncle Chet and the whole Brickyard Mike thing. Grams and Dad were able to hold them off, but the lawyers will give you a call later today about a meeting."

"I don't feel so good," I said. My stomach was doing flip-flops. I needed to think. I added, "I never knew what Uncle Chester did. I sat in the reception area cut off from anything. I let people in and out. Opened the mail. Paid a bill or two and that was it. There weren't even any files to speak of. I was there for what, a month or so?"

"I'm sure you're fine with the office stuff. What about the other thing?"

"Oh Bill, I don't know. How I could have been so wrong? Brickyard looked just like the shooter, but when I touched his hand I knew it wasn't him."

"Shit, that sucks for him. Still, he was a bad man, he was going to hurt you and he was after you for some reason. You know what a pacifist I am but in certain circumstances there is no choice."

"I wonder how Murph is doing. The thought of him killing someone is so foreign. He isn't the typical cop or detective. He seems like a good guy."

"I'm sure there are a few."

I threw my pillow at him.

"What was that for?"

"What are insinuating?" I knew I wasn't going to like what he was about to say.

"You can do better than a cop. Think of all the baggage the man has to carry around with him by performing his job. Be careful."

"You know me. Guys never last long. This one is different, though. You should meet him."

"You never give anyone a chance. You really want me to meet him?" Bill asked rolling his eyes.

"I need to work on me before I get wrapped up with a man. I would like you to meet him. He'll be over in about fifteen minutes."

"I guess I can stick around. Why is he coming over?"

"He wants to talk."

"I'm sure he does." Bill paced around the room fidgeting. "Before he gets here I have a few questions for you."

"Okay. Ask."

"You were on the books right?"

"For most of my pay. Uncle Chet sometimes gave me cash for running errands."

"Oh boy. Hopefully it wasn't anything illegal. What kind of errands?"

"I dropped packages off at different places for him. Usually in mid-town."

"I'm sure the cops are going to want to hear about that. How much did he give you?"

"A hundred. He told me it was shopping money."

"That's all? I wouldn't worry about a hundred," Bill walked over to the kitchen and plunked a brownie on a plate.

"Great. Can't wait to tell them. I can hear myself saying, 'by the way officer, or is it Fed guy, my uncle had me make potentially illegal deliveries and I was so stupid I only got a hundred bucks for it.' Do you think I should keep quiet? I mean, I don't know what was in the package. I did it like once or maybe twice."

"When the lawyer calls later, get me up here and we'll do a conference call. Let them tell you what to say or what to not say."

"Okay."

"So back to the subject. What about a real job? What do you want to do?" He ate the brownie in two bites then plopped another on his plate.

"I don't know."

"Oh come on, what are some of the things you like to do?"

"I like fashion." I played with one of the pillows. The fabric was the softest velvet imaginable and the color was a luminous sea blue.

"No, you like getting dressed up. Fashion equates to being a slave to some jerk again, please stop with that crap. I'm going to say something that you're not going to like, but it needs to be said. Ever since your junior year in college you've changed. Once you started hanging out with Ashley and her friends you became a shallow, materialistic snot. That's not you. Living in Trump Tower, fashion assistant job? Give me a break. What about throwing clay and opening a studio or having pop up shows to sell your art? Or design. You were creating cool websites before Wordpress; writing code like it was your first language without being taught. You sucked at math yet could do complex animations and fantastic graphics. What ever happened to your website?"

"I still have the address just haven't paid for the hosting. Been busy."

"Busy with what? Feeling sorry for yourself because you're not with those stuck up bitches? Not one of them came to visit you in the hospital. Your friends that did come were your art friends from high school and art classes. It was all over the news and the papers, they couldn't have missed it."

Ouch, that was more than a slap in the face, it was a big time slap to the ego and his words stung more than I wanted to admit.

"No tell me what you really mean, Pugsley."

"Sticks and stones my wonderful sister. You can call me that stupid childhood nickname, but remember I got past it unscathed. Face it; those dumb girls are not even close to being in your league. Stop following after other people's dreams and go after your own."

"With what? I still owe Dad fifty grand and I don't have a job. I can't ask him for anything else. I'm living off him as it is, and look at what Beatrice did. I couldn't hold my head up if I take anything else from them anymore."

"I happen to know someone who can help finance a venture. It's not as simple as having money handed over to you. You need to come up with a business plan, a marketing plan and do all of the leg work."

"Who is going to give me money to start an art venture? Are you suggesting a crowd funding deal where I need to beg for money? I am not going to do that. And anyway, it's a long shot at best."

"Sister, sister, sister. Why do you always forget to look right in front of you? Look at yourself and see your own future. You see everyone else's. It's time you took a good look into your own heart."

"But how? I touch my own hand and nothing happens."

"You started to try and find out about your gift and the one person who could help, you pushed away."

I tried to speak but he was right. My mother's mother, our grandmother Fiona, did know how to use these powers. She was a seer, herbalist and medium. I found some info about her online one day while I was bored at work and was surfing the net trying to see if anything would appear for my mother. No mother, but an interesting grandmother. She worked with stars and was renowned for her accuracy. I pushed her away the last time I saw her. It was a shock to see her as it had been close to ten years since our last visit.

"What do you have to lose?" He got up and looked out the window.

"Do you think Fiona will speak to me after the last time?"

"You were a total bitch, but I think she'll come around. She gave me a note to give to you."

"You saw her?" My eyes popped as he continued. I raced over to him and pulled the note from his hand.

"She came to the hospital to see you. I went up with her late one evening. She didn't want to upset Dad."

"Oye. I'm afraid to read it." I juggled the piece of paper in my hand; afraid it would scorch my hand.

"Want me to read it to you?"

I took a deep breath, scratched at my throat. It was starting to itch. I hoped that was a good sign and the healing was beginning.

"Okay, but do it quick before I chicken out." I handed the note back to him and closed my eyes.

He began, "Tisha, I came as soon as I heard the horrible news. I didn't want to put any more burdens on your family so I didn't come in until everyone was out of your room late in the evening. I held your hand and sang some of the silly songs I used to sing to you and your brother when you were little. I tried as hard as I could to give you some of my strength so that you would heal as fast as you can. Your physical wounds will heal. The mental ones are the ones that concern me. I have so much to tell you about your gift. I pray in my heart that you will give me the chance to make things right and help you through this difficult time. You and your brother are the light of my life, even if it is from afar. Please find it in your heart to give me some time. Love, Fiona."

She added her phone numbers and an e-mail address.

I didn't have a choice. I would call her.

"Okay Bill. After Detective Murphy leaves I'll give her a call."

"Good. She's a fascinating lady," Bill walked over and kissed the top of my head, "I'll be downstairs if you need me."

Detective Murphy was due any minute. I didn't know what to expect. I knew he came to my room a few times while I was in the hospital so I took that as concern, but how far that went I wasn't sure. I'll admit it. I had a crush on him. The memory of what happened floated back to me. I visualized traveling to work on the train. Brickyard Mike appeared. He grabbed me and tried to force me into a utility closet. Detective Murphy appeared. I slammed my heel into Brickyard's foot as he began slicing at my neck. He lurched forward and Murph shot him. As he lay dying, I reached out and grasped his hand and learned he wasn't the killer. It was the one most frightening event of my life. I couldn't let it control me.

Pushing away the curtain on my entryway door, I watched as a dark blue Mustang pulled into the driveway. I jumped away from the window afraid of being caught spying. A few minutes later there was a knock on the door. I waited five seconds, took a deep breath, fixed my hair in the mirror next to the door and then opened it.

"Hi, Murph. Come on in," I said.

"Tisha, how are you? You look great."

He pulled a beautiful bouquet of wildflowers from behind his back.

"For you," he said.

"They're beautiful. Come in have a seat. I'll put these in water. Can I get you something? Cappuccino, espresso, tea, juice?"

He sat down on the sofa. "Cappuccino would be great if it's not too much trouble."

"No trouble at all. My father's wife bought me this cool new machine. I've been dying to try it out."

I hit a button and let the machine do its job. It made some whirling noises and rewarded me with a perfect cup. I hit the button again to make a cup for myself.

"It'll be a minute. How are you?"

"It's been rough. Sleep hasn't been my friend. I'm having a hard time with the shooting. I know what I did was justified. If I didn't do it you wouldn't be with us. It's just ... taking a life is too much for me. It's not what I believe in and not something I want to have to make a decision about again."

He looked in the air as he spoke. I could tell he hadn't had much sleep from the worry lines on his face that were very evident. Torment was the best way to describe his demeanor.

"Have you talked to anyone? A professional I mean?"

"Yes, but it hasn't been much help. There are things about me that I don't want to share. Especially with the police shrink. And then there are other secrets I've been keeping. It's complicated."

"I understand complicated." I walked over to the coffee maker and brought the two cups to the sofa. Handing him one cup, I sat next to him with mine.

"What do you mean?" he asked.

"May I take your hand?"

Never in my life had I asked anyone for their hand. Somehow this man had touched my soul and I needed to help him. He saved my life. I needed to help him save his own. He reached out to me and I took his hand in both of mine. I closed my eyes and took it all in. What I saw convinced me of what I had to do. This man was more than special. The energy spark between us kept my hand tingling. I released his hand and got up.

"Would you like a brownie?"

"Sure."

"How long have you had visions?" I asked.

"What?" He squirmed in his seat. He looked like I had caught him with his hand in the cookie jar. He didn't know what to say so remained quiet.

"I have them too. When I touch someone's hand I see their past, present and future. I don't understand it and have been trying to avoid it, but it came to a head with Brickyard. When I touched him, I knew he wasn't the killer. I need to learn more about this ability. I can do something with this if only I knew how. What is your gift?" I expected him to look shocked, but he wasn't. More like relieved.

"It's not that dramatic. I can't even explain it. I know things. It's not telepathic or maybe it's clairvoyant, but I know things. I knew I would meet you the day of the first shooting. I had another appointment and was almost off duty, but came to the scene almost as if you were calling to me. That's why Detective Nelson and I weren't in the same car. The day of your shooting, I found out your uncle was getting arrested by the Feds and didn't want you to get swept up in the sting operation. No one told me about the raid, I just knew. I also knew that Brickyard wasn't the killer. These thoughts or realizations or whatever the hell they are come to me. I can't explain it and I can't control it. Sometimes it's constant overload with visions all the time. Other times there will be nothing for months and months. I know who killed Mario DeVito. He's the victim you saw shot. I don't know the shooter's name yet, but he's also related to Brickyard. It's either a brother or a cousin. You see, Mario and Brickyard were cousins."

"Oh my God, that's his name. Mario's been coming to me. Can't you find the killer?"

"What do you mean coming to you?" His eyes widened and brows rose.

"Seems that I have visions of dead people. It used to be where I would see flashes of people. Kind of like shadowy people. They would be in front of me and then *poof* gone. With Mario, he walked up to me and asked me to help him."

"Is he here now?"

"No. I only talked to him once since the shooting. Maybe it's the pain killers I've been taking."

"If someone were listening to this conversation, they would think we both need some serious drugs." We both started laughing. The sound of his voice and the sparkle in his eye was reassuring. I could let my hair down and confide in him. It was refreshing to find someone else with similar abilities.

"Can you find this other cousin guy? At least then the real killer can be locked up."

"I'm suspended pending an internal investigation. My attorney says it's just routine because I was out of jurisdiction when I fired my weapon. I don't have access to any files."

"I can help. I can find anything on the net."

"I'm not putting you into any more danger. When I get reinstated, I'll find this bastard. Sorry for the language."

"Don't be. I've heard it before. What about your partner, can he help?"

"He's an idiot. I'm not a member of his fan club right now."

"Well, there is no harm in doing a simple name search. My computer is encrypted so there is no way to trace the search back to me."

"Even if we find a name, we can't do anything yet. They need evidence to bring the guy in." He finished his cappuccino, placed his cup down on the coffee table and inched closer to me.

"But maybe somehow we can connect the dots. There has to be a reason Mario was killed. If we can figure that out then maybe we can link it to Brickyard and Mario's unnamed cousin. They are all cousins right?"

"Maybe. Yeah, they are all related. I'm afraid for you, Tisha. Something is going to happen. I'm not sure what, but something."

"Great. Can you maybe elaborate?"

"I wish I could, but it doesn't work like that for me. Promise me you'll stay close to home. If you need to go out, take someone with you. If you can't find anyone, call me. I'll be happy to keep you safe."

"This place is a fortress. Dad and my brother are on the overprotective side. I'm not supposed to drive for another week."

"I noticed the security coming in. That's a good thing."

I jumped up and hurried into my bedroom. "Getting my laptop," I called back over my shoulder. I pulled my laptop out of its case. Noticing some papers on the floor, I picked one up. They were some random papers I kept inside the laptop bag. I hadn't used my laptop since before I was in the hospital. Someone must have been in my room. I pressed the intercom button next to my bed.

"Bill pick up," I shouted.

Murph ran in. "What's the matter?"

"Someone's been in my room," I said into the intercom and to Murph.

Before I could put the phone down Bill came barreling through the door. I introduced the two, but they had already met at the hospital.

Bill asked, "Why do you think the apartment was broken into?"

"Because I haven't opened my laptop since before I came home from the hospital. Those papers were always tucked inside the pocket of the case. You know me, I hate it when things aren't in their place."

Bill put his fingers to his lips signaling for us to remain silent. He went down to the garage and reappeared carrying what looked like a flat iron. He waved his apparatus around the room. When it buzzed he examined the area, searched and found what appeared to be two tiny silver discs. He brought both it the bathroom stomped them with his heel and flushed them down the toilet bowl. I attempted to speak, but he darted me a look that indicated silence was to be continued. He opened my laptop and typed in a few lines. Prying the case apart, he dislodged a clear pin-like object. He walked over to the kitchen sink, filled a glass of water and dropped the device into it. He then placed a piece of saran wrap over the glass and placed it in the microwave. Pressing the button he set the oven for three minutes.

"Okay, we're good," Bill declared.

Hands on hips, I paced. "What was that all about?"

"The apartment's been bugged and your laptop had a tracking device attached to one of the USB ports."

"But how? Why?" I sat back down.

"I'm going to go downstairs and check on the surveillance tapes. Must have been something when we were all at the hospital. Funny, I browsed through and the only thing I saw were workmen and Beatrice coming and going getting your place all redone." Bill got up and made his way to the door.

"If you don't mind, is it okay if I take a look with you?" Murph asked.

"Sure."

I watched as they made their way down the stairs. The sky was a gorgeous shade without a cloud in it, but my stomach was screaming a storm was on its way. I pulled out my cell phone. The message button indicated 47 messages. I didn't think I knew 47 people. I went through the list and realized the press was very interested in speaking with me. One name came up over and over. It was Ms. Sven: Barbara Gallant, sister to my former voyeurism lustee. We met when Sven, whose name is really Ken, and I witnessed a murder while on the train. Barbara slept through the incident. What could she want with me? I listened to one of her calls.

> *Tisha, so sorry to hear about what happened to you. I am a newscaster for WWGTK and am interested in doing a feature on what happened to you. Not one of those dumb stories, but one where I highlight what it feels like to face death. Something classy, like you. Call me.*

The other six calls from her were similar. She was insistent. Maybe if I talked to her, I could come to grips with the whole situation. Plus, she was a woman. Talking to Bill and Murph were good, but women are different than men and I did need a friend. I dialed her number.

"Barbra Gallant, reporter," she chimed into the phone.

"Hi Barbara, this is Tisha Adams. We met a few weeks ago on the train."

"Oh my God. How are you? How are you feeling?" I looked into the phone and squinted. Was this the same self-centered woman who was more concerned with her lipstick application than a murdered man?

"Getting there. What's up?"

"I'm the host of a new series that goes inside the heads of both victims and criminals. My producer and I thought it would be fabulous to get your inside scoop on what you were feeling when that awful man tried to kill you."

"I don't know," I answered. How could I tell her how I felt if I didn't know myself? Everything was still fresh, raw.

"How about we meet for an interview? I can come to you."

"Barbara, I'm still trying to work out the whole episode myself."

"Well, how about we meet and start talking about it. No cameras, no recordings, just two friends, one trying to help the other through a hard time." This was sounding like something I needed.

"Okay, but it needs to be away from the house. My brother is watching me like a hawk."

"I understand. The press is on your doorstep too."

"Yeah, but it looks like that's slowing down. They leave around ten and are back just after nine in the morning," I said.

"I like to go for a run in the morning. How about we get together for a walk?"

"Sounds good. I sure need some air."

"There's that arboretum in Oyster Bay."

"I don't think they open until nine. How about Bailey's? It's in Lattingtown on Bayville Road."

"Hmm, I didn't realize there was another one. I'll Google it. What time is good for you?"

"How about seven? Or it that too early?"

"Seven it is. See you tomorrow."

Walking into my bedroom and lying down, I wondered if I was doing the right thing. As long as she was not recording anything, I thought I would be okay. The gnawing feeling got worse. I rolled over and swallowed a painkiller. In a moment I was fast asleep.

CHAPTER 6

D id you ever wake up and not know where you were? I bolted up hearing noises from the other room. Looking around nothing was familiar. The curtains, a canopy above the bed I was in and a large armoire surrounded me. There were people talking in the next room. I shook my head and wiped my eyes. This was my room. This was my house. I have to stop taking those painkillers. They made me forget things and I knew I was going to need my wits about me.

Tiptoeing into the living room, I found Bill and Murph studying some photos.

"Hey sleepy head, didn't want to wake you up. How are you feeling?" Bill asked.

"A little out of it," I said sitting down on a chair, "Gotta lay off those pills. They make me crazy."

"I'll get you some Tylenol. Listen, Murph and I were looking through the tapes and I found these two pictures I wanted you to look at. Ready?" he asked shielding them from me.

"I guess." What was the big deal?

Bill brought the photos to me. He uncovered the two and placed them in my hands.

"Look familiar?"

"Shit. It's Brickyard. But how could he have gotten into this place? Murph shot him."

"Seems, Brickyard has a brother. A twin brother," Murph answered.

"That still doesn't explain what he was doing in here."

"There must be something much bigger than we realize going on. Your brother told me that the bugs he found as well as the tracer in your computer are very sophisticated. They can't be purchased online or at a local store. Both are military grade espionage tools."

"What the hell have I gotten myself involved in? How do you know all of this?"

Murph pointed to Bill, "Looks like Bill has the answer to that."

"I created both of those locators. The bugs are a few generations old so they could have come from a number of places. The tracers are new. Brand new. I only had two customers for those."

"And?" I asked getting up. "What is going on Bill? Am I in danger? Are you?"

"None of this makes any sense to me. I'm going to contact my clients and see if I can't make heads or tails of this. The one client won't be a problem. The other, well. Let's just say it won't be easy." He looked up at the ceiling. His eye started to twitch, a move that I hadn't seen in years.

"I don't think I want to know."

"That's all I can say for now. Let me think about how to handle this. If you need me, I'll be downstairs," Bill said. His shoulders were slumped and he padded down the steps instead of his usual leaping down two at a time.

I turned to Murph, "What's going on?"

"What is it your brother does?"

"He works for a think tank and a computer company. He creates robotic and computer components."

"Not sure about the connection, but I think this whole thing goes deeper than we think." He sat back into his chair deep in thought.

"What does the A stand for?" I asked.

I roused him from his contemplation, "What?"

"The A. Your business card reads A. Murphy. What's the A for?"

"You don't want to know." His smile was back.

"My given name was Morticia. Bill was named Gomez William and now goes by G. William on his card and Bill in person. It couldn't be worse than that."

"You are sworn to secrecy. Pinky swears." He held out his hand, pointing a pinky at me.

I took it and wrapped my pinky around his.

"Pinky swears. Now spill."

"Agamemnon. Named after a king in the Trojan wars. My parents fell into the family custom of naming all of the children with the letter A. They started running out of names and well, my mother loved reading about the Trojan wars and so that's my name."

"Yikes. Not much of a nickname for that."

"Yeah. Well that's why it's Murph. The only person who still calls me that name is my mother. Even my dad uses Murph."

"Okay, Murph. Where do we go from here?"

He gave me his best come hither look. I might be slow at some things, but there was not an inkling of doubt as to what he had in mind. I strolled over to him. He took my hand and drew me into his arms. If I am never kissed again, I will never forget the connection that surged between us.

CHAPTER 7

A knock at the door broke the magic between us. I released myself from Murph's embrace and answered the door.

"Hi Tisha. Thought I'd bring ya'll some food," Beatrice said wielding a large platter covered in tinfoil.

"Beatrice, thank you," I said opening the door wider to let her and her tray into the apartment. She walked over to the counter and placed the platter down. Remembering my attempt at reconciliation, I picked up the flower arrangement I made for her the previous day.

"I picked these for you yesterday. They'll open up in another day or so. I made the vase back in art school."

Her eyes lit up, "Oh how thoughtful. This is beautiful. I don't know what to say."

"Nothing needs to be said except, I'm sorry. I was overwhelmed with your gesture. I do appreciate all of the work you put into getting this place transformed."

"You're welcome. I needed to do something. I felt so awful with what happened to you and I felt out of place at the hospital."

"Still there was no excuse for my behavior."

"You went through some awful trauma. Probably some crazy hormones or maybe the pain killers they gave you for your wound made you unlike your true self."

I held my tongue. What the hell did hormones have to do with getting your throat slit open? Taking a deep breath I said, "You're right."

"We need to get to know each other better. How about as soon as you're feeling better, we have *girls' only* day out. We can get facials and manicures. Oh, it will be so much fun." She trailed off realizing that Murph was in the apartment and listening.

"Have you met Detective Murphy?" I asked.

"No. How do you do?" She extended her hand toward him.

"Hi," Murph said.

The door flung open and Bill appeared.

"Right on time for lunch," Beatrice said.

"Perfect. I mean perfect that you're here Beatrice not just the lunch."

Removing the tinfoil revealed an array of sandwiches, a bowl of salad and a plate filled with a delectable assortment of cookies. I opened a cabinet and set out plates, napkins and utensils. Opening the fridge I found some mineral water and lemons. I pulled out four and began slicing the lemon.

"Dig in everyone."

We arranged plates and sat down around the coffee table balancing plates on our laps.

"Beatrice, were you in the apartment when the work was being done?" Bill asked.

"Yes. I asked the men for a speedy job and I wanted everything perfect so I supervised. I only left when they were painting."

"Who did you use for the painting?" Bill asked.

"LV Painting. Your father went to school with the gentleman who owns it. Otherwise we would have had to wait weeks for someone else to come in."

"Okay. That's good. What about the furniture? Where did that come from?"

"Is there a problem?" she asked.

"Not sure. It looks like someone might be watching Tisha. Murph and I want to find out who has been around her and this apartment since the shooting."

"Oh my word. I hope I didn't do anything to cause this." She began twirling her hair around her finger.

"I'm sure it's nothing that you did," Murph said.

"Okay. Well, let me think. The furniture in the living room came from Anthropologie. To get it here on time, I had to hire my own freight company. The coffee, end tables and bathroom accessories are from Crate and Barrel. I brought them home from the store with me in your dad's SUV. The textiles and armoire are from my friend's antique shop in town. She had her people bring them here."

"Who did you use for a freight company?"

"I found one in the yellow pages. They're in Glen Cove."

"Do you remember the name?"

"I just looked it up on the internet. I probably have the receipt downstairs. Shall I get it for you?"

"After we finish lunch," Bill said.

We ate in silence for a while. Attempting to get conversation flowing on a neutral topic, I said, "Beatrice, this is the best chicken salad I've ever had. What's in it?"

She smiled and answered, "It's real simple. I mix together a ranch dressing with a Caesar dressing and then add chicken, celery and roasted red peppers. In the summer, it's divine on a tomato that's been hollowed out. The bread adds another dimension. I picked this loaf up at Rocco's bakery. That place smells like pure heaven. We don't have anything like that down where I'm from."

She got up and put her plate in the sink. "I'll be back in a sec."

"What do you think?" Bill asked Murph.

"I think that one of the movers somehow knew what was going on here and planted the bugs. The only question is *how*. They had to know beforehand what was happening here. Only a few people did know about the renovation. It would have to be narrowed down to the painters, the moving company, the antique shop, Beatrice and your father."

"Right. Let me think out loud. I can check with the painters. I used to ride around on my bike with Tom McGowan. His dad, Kevin, owns LV Painting. Most of those guys have been with him for ages, but will check if he had any recent new hires. I didn't realize the antique shop is still there. Again, the woman who owns it is a friend of our grams'. I can almost guarantee nothing there. The only other potential lead would be the moving company. They are notorious for hiring transients. But that still doesn't account for them knowing a way to get in here or that something was happening. Shit. I'll be right back."

Bill raced out the door and down the steps. I could hear some muffled cursing from the garage. He reappeared holding up a piece of paper.

"I guess with all of the turmoil, I overlooked this." He handed Murph a piece of paper.

"Security breach, telephone pole alert," Murph read aloud with a questioning look, "What does that mean?"

"I have all kinds of security on the house for a variety of reasons. Most having to do with the work that both my father and I do. My dad is one of the leading geneticists in the world. I've made my mark in the world of robotics and computer components. There are a lot of people out there that would love to get their hands on some of our work. I do some work from downstairs and so does my father. This is a warning sheet that was generated the first night Tisha was in the hospital. Someone placed a bug on the telephone pole on the street to try and intercept calls. It could be anywhere. It's triggered when any outside calls are made from this property."

"But Bill, I don't have a landline."

"You don't, but Dad and Beatrice do."

"And she would have been making calls to get this all put together," I said.

"And I neglected to take a look at my printer. Nothing ever came through before."

"I feel like I'm in the Twilight Zone," Murph said.

"Sometimes, so do I," Bill answered.

Beatrice reappeared, "Is it okay to come in?" she called from the cracked open door.

"Come on in," I answered.

"Here's all of the paperwork from the store and from the moving company. Also, just in case, here is the antique shop and the painter's numbers. I'm so sorry I might have put you in danger."

"Thanks. This will help," Murph said.

"Okay, I have to get going. Your daddy and I are headed to a dinner tonight and I have to get ready."

"Thanks again Beatrice," I said ushering her out of the room. Her voice and accent were beginning to grate on me and I didn't want to have another outburst.

"Okay sugar, remember our girls beauty date. I'll book it for Thursday, if you need anything holler."

"Great. I'll be hollering," I answered.

"Smooth," Bill added as she closed the door behind her.

"What else was I suppose to do? Maybe we can make it a family outing. Need the boils blown off your butt?"

"Nice mouth," Bill said.

I forgot Murph was there. He seemed amused with my humor and tried to hold back the laughter.

"Sorry Murph. She and I don't see eye to eye. I think it's the southern talk thing. All that sugar, ya'lling and hollering makes me want to scream."

"I hear you," he said adding, "We have to find out what the hell is going on."

Bill shuffled through the papers Beatrice gave him. He pulled out his cell and dialed a number mouthing, *the moving company.*

"Yes, good afternoon. Last week I had some furniture delivered to my home. No, no everything went well. You see my wife isn't from around here. They have different customs from where she came, and it seems she neglected to tip the fine young men who brought the pieces in. I was hoping I could swing by and give them a gratuity. Yes, I'll hold," Bill covered the mouthpiece. "She's looking it up on the computer," he continued his conversation, "it was last Wednesday, we're at 890 Piping Rock Road in Locust Valley, Adams is the name. Fantastic, I'll swing by later."

He ended the call with a wide grin lighting up his face.

"George Fallon, Billy Dempsey and James O'Sullivan. Mean anything?"

"Brickyard Mike's last name was O'Sullivan," Murph answered.

"Now what do we do?" Bill asked.

"We still don't have anything. At least nothing to warrant a search or even questioning. I'm suspended so I can't even call on them."

"I can still go down and tip them," Bill said.

"You're asking for trouble. Let me call one of the guys I was tight with. Maybe I can get him on board."

"If someone is listening in on phone calls going in and out of the house, this, whatever the this is, isn't over. I'm not going to sit here and do nothing. We need to find out what the hell is going on and stop it."

Murph looked from my brother to me. "You're right."

"I'm going down to the moving company. They get off work at four. I gotta get there before then." Bill made his way toward the door.

"Hold up. I'm going with you."

I looked from one to the other, "Are you both insane? This guy could be dangerous. He might have killed the dead guy. I mean Mario. If they're tapping phones, he's not finished."

"I carry a gun and on the way over I'll call John. He's the one detective I can trust."

"Okay, but as soon as you finish, call me. My stomach is already in my throat."

Murph leaned in and kissed me, "Don't worry. We'll be fine."

Bill's raised his eyebrows and did his best not to make a snide comment.

"Back in a few," Bill said.

I watched them go down the stairs, get into Murph's Mustang and drive away. My stomach was growling, but I was unable to get a good read on why. I didn't know if it was a premonition or the havoc the pain meds were playing on my stomach. I decided I would listen to Bill and switch over to

Tylenol rather than the prescription drugs. I needed to keep my wits about me and get into tune with my gift.

I sat down on the sofa and put my feet up. Shutting my eyes I tried to take a nap, but sleep wouldn't come. I was worried about the guys. I pulled on a sweater and walked outside. It was a crisp day, the sun was shining and a breeze was blowing from the north keeping the temperature cool. I headed to the back of the property to a pond that abutted the nature preserve next door. As a child this was one of my favorite places to sit. There was a bench made of stone and wood with a natural canopy thanks to the weeping willow tree whose wispy branches shaded the sunlight. I sat down and the fairy friends of my childhood appeared as they always had when I was at a crossroad. They frolicked around the pond dancing with delight, their cherub faces smiling and laughing. Joining hands the group encircled me chanting a sweet melody. I knew this was a good sign. They were my protectors keeping an eye out and warning me of danger. If all was well, they played in their carefree joyous way. If it wasn't, they'd give me a sign. I needed to trust my instincts and let these imps guide me. I needed to come to terms with my gift and find out how it could help me.

CHAPTER 8

T he sound of the security gates opening and the hum of a car approaching brought me back from my trance. I walked toward the driveway to see Murph and my brother getting out of Murph's car. They parked in front of one of the garage bays. I wondered why we used the garage as a workshop and art studio and the old stables as the garage. Guessing the proximity to the house was the reason. I filed the thought in my brain. It was a question for Dad.

"Hey, lady. How are you feeling?" Bill asked.

"The air feels good. Being cramped up in the hospital drained me," I said stretching.

"Well, we have good news and we have bad news," Murph said.

"Do tell."

"James O'Sullivan only worked one day. The day furniture was delivered to the house, but he left a cell number and it's a good one."

"Did you call him?" I asked smiling.

"No. Calling would alert him that we're on to him. We're going to track him and see where it leads. Then I'll hand it over to Detective Nelson and he'll make the collar," Murph said.

"Why do you want to track him?" I asked.

"This thing goes deeper than what we're seeing. The murder you witnessed doesn't make sense on many levels. Something else is going on. Why are they spying on you? We can't arrest him and I'm afraid if we question him, he'll disappear, but there will still be a danger out there."

"Okay, are we talking conspiracy?" I asked.

"Maybe. I'm not sure yet," Murph said.

"I'm lost. This is too much for my weak brain to handle."

"Do you ever go with your gut? You told me about the gift you have when you touch people. I told you about how sometimes I know things. There is more here than a random or even crime-related murder. Our guy was killed because he knew something. Whoever is doing this wants to learn something from you or this household. That's what we need to find out."

"Bill, what do you think?"

"Not sure it makes sense or if I can help." Scratching his head he made his way to the garage.

"Let's go inside and create a plan of action. We need to brainstorm about who this Mario guy was, what he knew and why he was better off to these people dead. And then, we need to find out the connection between them and my family. I think I'm going to be sick," I said.

"Don't be afraid. No one is going to harm you," Murph said giving me a squeeze.

"No, you don't understand. I think it was something I ate or the meds. I'll be back in a sec."

I raced up the stairs and ran to my bathroom. I purged myself. Brushing my teeth, I thought about what Murph was implying. It made me wonder why anyone would want to be a police officer and chase after criminals putting yourself in harm's way. I was afraid and I didn't think I could do it. I made it to my bed and collapsed. Sleep enveloped me.

CHAPTER 9

"**G**oing to call her?" Bill was sitting at the end of my bed.

"What time is it? I'll call in the morning, I guess."

"It's nine-thirty. Why not now?" He pulled the pillow from beneath my head.

"I'm tired and I got to get up my nerve. I'll be better in the morning." I let out a fake yawn and rubbed my eyes.

Bill pulled out his phone and dialed a number, "Hi Fiona, I'm here with Tisha, she'd like to talk to you."

I was shaking my head like a mad woman. I wanted to run and hide. The last encounter I had with my grandmother was anything but cordial. I didn't want to take the phone but I had little choice.

"Hello," I said.

"How are you feeling? You sound good for all that you've been through."

"I'm okay. Tired and sore." I wracked my brain trying to think of what to say next but it was blank.

"I won't keep you. How about we meet out at my place, say next week? Will you be able to drive or would you like me to come to you?"

"I think it would be best for me to go to you. I should be okay next week. I go to the doctor on Friday for follow-ups."

"How's Tuesday, say lunchtime?"

"Sure." I itched my throat.

"Bill said he was coming too. He'll give you directions. And bring Murph if you'd like. If you need anything before then, I'm here for you. Please call at any time."

"Okay. Well, I need to take a nap."

"Sleep well my angel."

That tore me up. When I was a little girl she always called me her little angel. I believed that I really was an angel.

"Now that wasn't hard was it?" Bill said sporting an *I told you so* look.

"You're such a shit."

"But you wouldn't have called. Move forward right? Confronting your past is part of moving forward."

"Well it's set. We're going to her house on Tuesday. Will the car make it out there?"

"The Smart car is a fantastic car, I don't understand why you hate it so much."

"I barely fit in it, plus I'm afraid I'll be squashed if I get in an accident."

"It's safe, you'll be fine."

"So you told her about Murph? She asked that I bring him. Where does she live?"

"Don't you remember? She lives out on the beach in San Remo. I didn't say a word about Murph."

"I thought maybe she might have moved. Funny, oh wait; she said she came late at night to visit, maybe she ran into Murph then."

"She didn't move, it's the same house we visited a few times years ago. Yeah, maybe she met Murph at the hospital."

I thought about the trips out to see grandmother. We'd sing silly songs along the way. My dad liked taking the local roads so we'd head out onto Route 25A and continue through Huntington, Northport and then to Smithtown. We'd head north on Old Dock Road and take it all the way to the end traveling on a long winding road to a lovely home that resembled a small castle. It was made of stone, covered in ivy with a lush green lawn surrounding the house. Down a few hundred yards was the Nissequogue River and a little further the opening to the Long Island Sound. The view was spectacular. The two of us would squeal in delight as we ran around and down to the water, plunging ourselves into the cold water, yelping as children do. Those days were filled with parties; dozens of people and lots of children followed by an enormous feast and the evening would be capped off with bonfires, marshmallow roasts and music. There was always music. I forgot about those wonderful carefree days. I was a very young, but I could still smell the salty air, hear the soulful music and taste those sublime marshmallows. I had been too hard on my grandmother. She was a victim of association. We were all victims. I could let it ruin me or face it and let it raise me up.

"I'm going back to sleep. Staying?"

"Yeah, I think you need supervision. I'm going downstairs to check on my equipment in the garage. I can do some work and then I'll be back up. Call out if you need me, I'll keep the intercom on."

"Thanks Bill. You're the best. Oh crap. Where's Murph?"

He gave me a hug. "He left hours ago. Maybe I was wrong about him. We need to figure out what's going on." I could see he was choked up.

"We will and I promise to get my act together."

He laughed, "Good because I can't stay here forever. The sofa is very chic, but it wasn't made for sleeping on. I'm beginning to miss my own apartment and bed."

I feel back asleep to a peaceful dreamless sleep.

CHAPTER 10

Waking, I glanced at my clock noting it was just after six. Stretching, I rolled on my side and got out of bed. I didn't like the queasy feeling I was having. Chalking it up to the previous day's stomach upheaval, I marched into the bathroom to shower before I met with Barbara. My stomach continued to roll as if I were on a rowboat in the middle of the Atlantic during a hurricane. The cup of ginger tea I drank didn't help nor did the antacids I was popping like they were skittles. I needed some fresh air.

I drove the few short streets to the arboretum. Turning into the drive, the parking lot was obscured by the long stables that had been transformed into an educational center. The only other car in the lot was another Smart car. Funny, given the choice of cars, that wouldn't be in the top ten on my list. Perhaps with her job in the city, Barbara chose it for its ability to maneuver and park almost anywhere. I'd be afraid to drive it into Manhattan. I shuttered thinking about how cabbies and trucks would have a field day cutting her off or even not seeing her and possibly running her over while she was sitting in her own car.

I parked and got out of my car. Walking around, I didn't see a soul. The spring air was cool on my face and the scent of forsythia welcomed me. Making my way toward the walking path, I saw what looked like a trail on the ground. It was bright red. Trying to make sense of it, I followed the trail trying to understand why a red paint trail would be on the ground. Maybe it was some sort of game.

But something was off. My heart was racing. Sweat was accumulating on my brow. I slowed my pace as I came to a turn. Peering around the curve my worst fear was realized. At first I thought I was looking at a pile of rags on the side of the trail. I approached, trying not to comprehend what lie in front of me. As I got closer my heart sank. Not again. *What the fuck is going on?* It was a body. Barbara's body.

I pulled out my phone and dialed 911.

"What's your emergency?" the stern voice on the other end asked.

"I found a body at the arboretum," I answered.

"A body?"

"Yes."

"What is your location?"

I walked a little closer. The body moved. I jumped back.

"Holy shit," I screamed, "I think she's alive. She's moving. Please get an ambulance down to Bailey's Arboretum. I'm about a hundred feet in on the path around the first turn. Please, help."

"Do you want me to stay on the phone with you? Do you see anyone else there?"

"No, I'm going to try to help her, please hurry."

I knelt down to her side and asked, "Barbara, can you hear me?"

She was on her side and tried to open her eyes. Not answering, she let out a moan. I tried to remember my CPR class. I looked to see where or if there was an obvious wound. I didn't want to move her. Examining her further I could see a big gash on her chest. I was afraid to start CPR for fear I would make her injuries worse. I reached down and held her hand.

I babbled for her to stay with me, to be strong, that help was on the way.

Her eyes rolled back into her head. I shouted, "You can do this. They won't hurt you anymore, you'll be safe. The ambulance is coming. Hear that? They're on the way. Barbara hold on."

Her eyes opened pleading with me to make what I said to her be true. We both knew that wasn't the case. I heard the wail of sirens and stood when I saw the group of volunteer firefighters and EMTs run around the curve. They tried to help. It was too late. She left this world the moment they arrived. Her dead eyes stared up at the sky seeing nothing.

I knew what happened to her as I held her hand. I could see the shock, the torment, the pain she endured after being shot in the chest and left to die in the woods like a piece of trash. It made me angry that one person could be so callous, so disrespectful of human life. I knew I needed to help her and I was afraid. Afraid of who did this to her and afraid that the police were going to think I was somehow involved if I told them what I knew.

Another emotion put my fear in check. It was rage. Barbara didn't know who her killer was or why she was shot. I was the target. We drove the same type of car. We were tall, slim and blonde. This was meant for me. I wasn't going to let it happen again. I didn't want anyone else hurt and I sure as hell didn't want to die.

The police arrived. I didn't say anything except how I found her. I was glad we were at a shielded part of the park obscured from onlookers. The last thing I needed was prying eyes or stupid gawkers. I sat on a bench trying to take my eyes off of this destroyed woman but couldn't. I felt responsible. Whoever was after me was not going to get away with this. I was determined. When the coroner arrived, I watched as they loaded her lifeless body into a large black bag. The sound of the zipper was an eerie reminder of the zipping away of a life.

After what seemed like hours, I returned to my little car and putted home. Glancing down at my phone, I had fourteen calls. I didn't want to answer any of them. The need for my safe warm bed and its covers hiding my body from the rest of the deranged world was overwhelming. How the hell was I going to walk away from this, walk away from that poor woman? I failed at finding the other killer and I saw him. How would I ever figure out who shot the life out of this poor soul?

CHAPTER 11

T he next few days passed in a blur. I slept, went to doctor's and slept some more. Beatrice was cooking up a storm, bringing me food at regular intervals. I had a hard time saying no. My pants were starting to get tight and the last thing I wanted was to go up a size. Bill worked incessantly. I knew he was working because he had a habit of yelling at his robots when they didn't do what he wanted. He treated them like pets. They gave me the creeps. I stayed away from the garage. Life seemed to be going on like it normally did. Everyone's life ... but mine.

Today was Barbara's funeral and I felt compelled to attend. I showered and dressed in a dark dress and low-heeled pumps. Adding a scarf to conceal my neck, I took a peek in the mirror at myself and was not happy at what looked back at me. A haggard, tortured woman was staring back. I sat down and waited for Bill to collect me for the drive to the church. Closing my eyes, I tried to take in some deep breaths to relax my agitated state. Opening my eyes, I found I wasn't alone.

Across from my chair, seated on the sofa was the dead guy, Mario, and beside him was Barbara.

"What's going on?" I whispered.

"Oh you don't need to be so dramatic," Barbara said. "We need your help."

"Your buddy Mario told me that, but I don't know how. How do I help you? What happened? Who killed you?" I was going mad. The people with the nets were going to come for me and lock me away in some musty loony bin with all the other crazies.

"That's what we need for you to find out. Seems like you're next on Mario's killer's list. The two murders are connected. We can't go over to the other side until this is resolved." Barbara kept flipping her hair. I wanted to reach out and stop her, but how do you grab a ghost?

"Why doesn't Mario talk?" I looked at Mario. "You need to tell me what you know."

"Can't. I swore to them to keep my mouth shut," Mario answered darting his eyes around the room.

"What? They killed you. You don't owe them anything." Was I really having this conversation? I was certifiable.

"A blood oath is a blood oath. I'm no snitch."

"Your allegiance is commendable, but remember you came to me not the other way around. Now spill."

"Can't." He folded his arms across the gaping hole in his chest.

"Okay. What *can* you tell me?"

"I'm Mario DeVito, 28, and I live in Howard Beach, alone. I have one sister and a shitload of cousins. My mom still lives in the house I grew up in. My dad died a long time ago. Same way as me."

I thought I'd try some reasoning. "Don't you think your mother would want to find out who killed her only son?"

"That's enough." He disappeared.

"What the fuck? Barbara, please tell me what to do." I got up and started pacing. The sweat dripped down my back and I was close to hyperventilating.

"Calm down. Take it step by step. Everything is connected and it somehow leads back to you. You can do this. I can only go so far. Do you have any idea what it took to get Mario to come with me?"

"He came to me weeks ago, why is he clamming up now?"

"Not sure, but I won't stop talking. Whoever did this cut me down before I could realize my dreams. That's not fair. I was only twenty-three and had it all. I could have been the next Barbara Walters. I know I would have. Can you help me?"

"Will you leave me alone if I do?"

Barbara jumped up and ran over to me, her outstretched arms trying to give me a hug, but she vanished before she reached me.

The door opened and Bill appeared.

"You don't look so good. Are you sure you want to go to this thing?" His eyes were filled with concern.

"Let me splash some water on my face. I'll be fine. Tomorrow it's off to Fiona's and boy do I need her."

CHAPTER 12

My father insisted on more security than the police were willing to provide and brought in a team to maintain a presence at the house as well as drivers to take us where we needed to go. Bill and I drove with our new driver, Marco, and bodyguard, Curtis, to a church in Glen Head on the main drag. The day was picture perfect spring with trees plumed out in various shades of light green and flowers waking from their winter slumber starting to dazzle the eyes with their vibrant color. Not a cloud or even a chem trail marred the sky. Barbara would approve.

Cars were stacked one behind the other on both sides of the street. Police directed traffic attempting to rein in the mob and media set up their cameras at the entryway to the church. I should have felt like a celebrity with my entourage and sleek new limo, but all I could feel was dread and despair. The thought that kept running around in my head was why was I being targeted and how did it fit in with the shooting I witnessed on the train?

Taking a deep breath, I took Bill's hand as he helped me out of the car. Curtis had performed a recon of the area scanning the street, talking into a headset and scooting us into the church through a side door before the media could assault us. Curtis assured us there would be other security at the church before we arrived to be sure no harm came to me. The large old Romanesque church was bustling with the sound of the living. Somber music played in the background, audible yet muted compared to the lively discussions in the pews. We made our way halfway down to the nave and found a pew for the three of us to sit. I did something I never did. I knelled down and said a prayer. I recited the Lord's Prayer and then a Hail Mary. I needed all the help I could get.

The organ rang out quieting the crowd. The congregation rose. As the music played the funeral march, the procession began. A white coffin covered with pink roses was wheeled down the aisle followed by the grieving family. Ken had a difficult time standing upright and was helped by two men I guessed were relatives with their similar tall, blonde and handsome features. His body was wrought with grief, his face a drug-induced blank and his affect beaten. Our eyes met for a moment. I tried to send some positive vibes, but he was beyond consolation. I felt his pain, his loss.

The priest made his way to the pulpit and conducted his sermon. My thoughts wandered. Something wasn't right. That little voice inside my head that screams danger was activated. I couldn't ignore it. I gave Bill a nudge and tapped Curtis on the shoulder.

"We have to leave," I whispered to Bill.

"Are you okay?" he asked.

"No. Something is wrong. I have to get out of here."

Curtis led us out to the vestibule. He dialed the driver. Nothing. He tried again. No answer. He called his team, but again no answer.

"What the hell is going on?" Bill asked.

"I don't know. Let's see if there's a landline we can use. Stay close," Curtis said.

The three of us walked down the corridor and found a staircase leading to the basement. We crept down the stairs leading us to a locked door. Curtis took something out of his breast pocket and fiddled with the lock. The door opened.

Another hallway and stretch of doors greeted us. Searching through a few rooms with opened doors, Bill found a telephone. Curtis picked it up and smiled.

"It's working. I'm calling base." He dialed and waited a moment. Continuing he said, "Guard S1 trying to get to TC1, no response."

Minutes passed. My stomach was flipping. I needed to pay my respects to Barbara by attending this funeral, but my gut screamed *mistake*. My guilt was overshadowing my reasoning and my abilities. I was hollow. Maybe I was all wrong and the intended victim was Barbara. But that didn't explain our inability to contact the driver.

"Okay, got it. There is a rear exit. From the floor plan of the church, I think we can make it from our current location without being seen. Yes, will do." Curtis hung up the phone and said to us, "Looks like the Feds blocked all the cell channels in the vicinity. Could be for this or it might be something going on nearby. Barbara was working on a few stories, all of them tied to unsolved murders; a few of them involved questionable characters. The car is circling around and will meet us out back. There are six team members keeping watch. When they give me the nod, we'll make our way to the car. Marco will get as close as he can."

"Should we run?" I asked.

Curtis laughed, "You'll be fine. We're here so that nothing happens to you and your brother."

"I know and appreciate it, but this is way out of my comfort zone. I want my boring life back."

"Don't worry. Everything will be okay."

We made our way up another stairway and hung back as Curtis poked his head out the door. He made some hand signals to an unseen person and shook his head.

"Okay, it's clear." He bolted out the door and pulled open the latch on the car as it pulled up, hugging the side of the building. We jumped in as instructed and sped off.

"I want my bed," I said taking a deep breath.

"We'll be home soon," Bill said stroking my hair.

"Will anything ever be the same? What the fuck is going on?"

"Don't worry Tisha. Dad and I are going to keep you safe. We'll find out what's going on and we can all get back to a normal life."

I put my head on his shoulder closing my eyes, wanting to believe him.

CHAPTER 13

The day of reckoning arrived. Searching through my armoire, I tried to find the perfect outfit. Clothes were strewn about the room; possible outfits hung on the doors, flat and lifeless until I tried them on. Nervous was an understatement. My grandmother Fiona was a distant memory from a childhood full of unanswered questions. Perhaps today I could understand what happened to my mother, why I can see things when I touch another person's hand, and most important, what I can do when and if I find out more about this gift. I needed for the hole in my heart to be filled with answers, not the shutting down of questions that was my father's way of not dealing with missing solutions that eluded him.

Settling on a pair of *7 for All Mankind* dark-wash skinny crops, Vince d'Orsay grey snakeskin flats and a vintage white gauze top; I checked myself in the mirror. Not bad. I tossed the scattered clothes on one chair and smoothed my duvet. Thinking about the beachside home, I pulled open a dresser draw and rummaged for a wrap. Finding an Aztec print cashmere, I put it next to my bag and was ready to go. Pushing back the curtain on the front door, I gazed out to see if Murph had arrived. To my horror, the security team was patting him down, had all of his car doors open and was searching his car. I threw the door open and stood on the landing.

"What the hell are you guys doing?"

"Our job, miss. Please step back inside," the lead, a Rock lookalike, called out to me in a *no I'm not taking any of your shit* kind of way.

Retreating into my cell, I sat at the counter waiting for Murph to be admitted. This had to end. I couldn't take much more.

A tap on the door and the knob slowly turning, Murph let himself in. He had an amused grin. "Never thought I'd be the one getting frisked," he laughed.

"I'm so sorry. I had no idea they were going to do that." I got up and went to him. Reaching out I drew him in close to me hugging him and looking up to kiss him. Our lips met and I was far, far away from this nightmare and into the land of fireworks and sunsets.

He stepped away, "If we keep that up we'll never get out of here. I have plans for later." He stepped back sending me a sheepish grin.

"Oh, do tell," I said.

"Then it wouldn't be a surprise. You look beautiful." His eyes admired me and I couldn't help but blush. Boyfriends didn't last long. After reading their thoughts, my interest would poof out like a birthday cake candle. This chemistry was something else. It was beautiful.

"Thank you. You are looking pretty good yourself." I was almost right. He was dressed in jeans that revealed a wonderful butt, a blue button down and was carrying his navy sport jacket on his arm. His soulful eyes revealed a lack of sleep and a lot of concern.

"Ready?" he asked.

"Looking forward to this. I'm a little afraid, but it's time to get some insight on what happens to me. Onward. Our limo awaits."

"Limo? I was going to drive."

"Do you want to get manhandled again?"

"No. Getting felt up by a guy is not my idea of a good time. He can drive."

"Marco is the driver. Curtis is the bodyguard."

"A chaperon too? I am a cop."

"Murph, with everything that's going on it's probably a good idea."

"You're probably right. It tugs at my manhood."

"Well maybe later, something else will be tugging at your manhood." I giggled.

"Keep that talk up and we won't be going anywhere." He took a step closer to me.

"Off we go," I said as I ducked and ran past him. Turning back around, "Coming?"

"You are one mean lady. Yes, I'm coming."

Rather than traversing the scenic North Shore, Marco opted for the LIE, Sunken Meadow parkway route. Not much to look at other than cars and road signs. Instead of outward, I was focusing inward, trying to relax and hoping at least a few of my questions would be answered. Murph also seemed to be contemplating. Sitting close, I felt his warmth. Although not wearing cologne, he had a spicy scent to him. I reached out to take his hand, but he pulled away. He gave me a mischievous grin. Ahhh, I guess this time I would be left in the dark.

Making the final turn toward Fiona's house was like going back in time. The house with its fieldstone façade and towering turrets could have been from a medieval castle. All it was missing was a moat. The Long Island Sound sparkled in the distance while the house seemed to be illuminated by the specks of quartz in the regal stone and the way the sun reflected off of it. Curtis got out of the vehicle and did his recon. We sat waiting for him to return with the all clear sign. I didn't imagine it would take long since the house was at the end of the road without any other in sight.

"I don't think I will ever run for political office," Murph said.

"What?" I looked at him trying to understand what he was talking about.

"The security. Can you imagine being like the president and having to go through this every day? Having to be suspect of everyone around you. Afraid to turn a corner because someone might be there who wants to blow your head off."

"Where is that coming from? Why did you ever decide to be a cop? The more I get to know you, the more it seems like it is not a job for you."

"I've had a lot of time to think. More than the suspension. I became a cop because my father is a cop. His father was a cop and all of the men in the family are cops."

"Family tradition?"

"More like family curse. There are better ways to make a living."

"I suppose there are. Any ideas?"

"I'm working on something."

"Do tell," I said wondering what this gorgeous man beside me was thinking. As he was

about to speak, the car door opened.

"It's all clear. It's safe to go in," Curtis said.

He held his hand on the car door as I got out of the limo. Murph followed as we walked up the wide stairway to the front door. I rang the bell and smiled at the chiming of the bells singing their sweet melody. The massive double doors opened and Fiona appeared.

"Come in," she called, stepping aside to let us inside. She was dressed in a flowing white gauze dress that skimmed her ankles, her long platinum hair tied with a loose navy ribbon and silver earrings accented with cobalt blue stones. She embraced me and gave me a quick peck on the cheek. She reached out for Murph's hand and pulled him in closer giving him a hug. "Thanks for keeping my angel safe," she said.

"Thanks for having us ma'am," he said.

"Please call me Fiona."

"Okay, Fiona."

We stood for a moment, each of us looking at the other.

"I've waited for this day for so long and now I've turned into a blithering idiot. Come on in. How about we sit down and get to know each other."

Fiona led us down a long hallway past an impressive marble stairway and through the kitchen to an atrium. Although the walls were glass it was difficult to see through them with all of the plants the room housed. There were herbs of all variety planted directly in a raised bed surrounding the perimeter. What appeared to be grape vines traversed the metal structure of the room. Lemon and lime trees heavy with fruit and bursting with heavenly scented flowers were lined up surrounding a table and chairs. Orchids of more types than I could count were scattered about the room on stands, hanging from pots and tucked into the crook of a small tree, their unique flowers a visual delight. What appeared to be a sort of aquaponic system was filled with an assortment of greens while fish swam below it in a large glass tank. There was so much going on it was hard to take it all in.

"Please have a seat. The atrium is bursting at the seams. Everyone is ready to go out for the summer, but I think we need another week or so to be on the safe side. This close to the sound can be unpredictable and I wouldn't want any harm to come to my babies. I was going to make a pot of tea to start. How does that sound? Bill not able to make it?" She motioned to a table set for four with pure white china, crystal champagne flutes and sparkling silver cutlery.

"Wonderful! No Bill had a deadline to meet. He said he'd call you later this week," I answered.

"Tea sounds great," Murph added.

"I hope you weren't put off by the security guy. His name is Curtis. You know Dad. Mr. Overprotective," I said as Fiona was making her way toward the kitchen.

"No, not at all. I understand his concern. Plus I was expecting it. Beatrice called before you arrived. I'll just be a sec."

I turned to Murph mentally scratching my head. "I haven't seen Beatrice in a few days. She and Dad are at one of his conferences. How would Beatrice know where we were going? And aren't the phones still bugged?"

"Maybe Bill said something to her." Murph was busy studying the room. He got up and took a closer look at the herbs. "This room is incredible. It's like a small farm. Wait a minute. Beatrice is gone. How would she know anything?" His eyes widened. "Where is your cell phone?"

I opened my purse and pulled it out. "Here it is."

He motioned for me to give it to him. He pulled the back cover off and searched the mechanics. Finding what he was looking for, he removed a tiny round disc.

Fiona rejoined us carrying a large tray. Murph put his finger to his lips signaling not to talk. He walked through the French doors and down toward the beach. We watched as he picked up a rock and crushed the disc with another. He walked about on the beach looking down. Finding what he was looking for he picked up what appeared to be a bottle and tossed it into the sea. He made his way back to us and sat down.

"What's going on?" Fiona asked.

"Too much. So when the heck was that bug added to the mix? What the hell does this person want from me?"

"It appears that Tisha is the target of someone. We think it may have to do with her job, but it also could be related to the murder she witnessed," Murph said.

"Murder, your job ... this doesn't make any sense. Can you start from the beginning?" Fiona asked.

I went through the short version. My grandmother's face went from a cheerful, healthy smile to a ghastly pale-faced horror.

"I need to make a call," Murph said when I finished my bizarre story. He got up and walked outside.

Fiona turned to me. "We'll get to the bottom of this. I can't understand how people can be so callous and greedy that they have no regard for life and use people like their pawn in some sick game. Two people dead. It breaks my heart. And you poor child, having to witness both of them one right after the other. You're here now. I can help."

"I sure hope you can. On top of that, both the victims have come to me."

"What do you mean?" She leaned in closer toward me.

"At first it was just the dead guy. His name was Mario. Mario DeVito. He came to me at the train platform in Queens and I think he was following me before he made himself known to me. He asked me to help him. After I was attacked nothing, but then two days after Barbara was killed both of them appeared. Barbara seemed to still be with us. Mario was reluctant to talk. Barbara said she'd try to persuade him to tell her what happened. She doesn't want her killer to be loose. He doesn't feel the same claiming he took an oath not to snitch." I sat back in my chair and thought about what I said. I think I needed to think about checking myself into a mental institution. This was not rational or sane.

"When they came to you what were you thinking about?" Fiona didn't seem to be phased by my admission.

"Let me think. On the platform, I was kicking back thinking about doing some shopping before meeting with Murph and Ken. When Barbara and Mario came together, I had just woken up." The wheels were turning.

"And what does that tell you?" Fiona asked.

"That it happens like randomly?"

"No, try again."

"Okay," I looked up at the sky. Perhaps that would help since this whole thing was like reaching for a star, way beyond my grasp. Then it clicked, "I was relaxed. I wasn't thinking about anything."

"Got it," Fiona smiled.

The doors opened and Murph took his seat. "I called Detective Nelson and let him know what I found. He was pissed I didn't save it, but I never saw a bug like that and didn't want to take any chances. After smashing it with the rock, I found a bottle by the shore. The crushed device should be on its way to Connecticut by now."

"How could another person have gotten into the house after Dad brought in all the security?"

"When Bill was doing the search, he didn't ask for your cell phone."

"You're right, but if the other bugs were put in at the house when I was at the hospital, when did they put this one in? The phone was in my purse with me at the hospital."

"You were unconscious and heavily medicated. Anyone could have walked into your hospital room."

Fiona was listening and shaking her head. "This is too much for me. Murph where are the police in the investigation?"

"Right now, not very far along. Mario DeVito had ties to organized crime. Brickyard Mike, whose name is really Michael O'Sullivan, was his cousin and also a known as a hit man among other things. The police are looking to question Mike's twin brother, Kevin, but they can't find him. Tisha's Uncle Chester was arrested. He was bailed out and now is also nowhere to be found. When I called Nelson a few minutes ago, he told me the weapon used to kill Barbara Gallant was an assault rifle fired from the third floor of the main house at the arboretum. The shooter knew what he was doing. It's still not clear who was the intended target. Barbara Gallant had been ruffling feathers by trying to get an exclusive on a story, any story, to make a name for herself. There isn't any security system in place at the arboretum, only a locked door that was jimmied."

"Some good it did her," I said thinking about my conversation with her.

"When she came to me she wasn't able to give me anything. She doesn't know who shot her."

"They're clearly looking to you for help Tisha," Fiona said.

"But how can I help?"

"It's easy. You simply need to practice."

I looked to Murph and he to me, both of us shrugging our shoulders.

"Why don't we go inside so we can sit back on some comfortable chairs?" Fiona led us into the house bringing us to a cozy sitting room. Four tapestry wing chairs were angled to face a large marble fireplace. A kilim rug graced the floor sitting atop rich oak planks.

"I love this room. It's a great place to contemplate and connect. Please sit," she pointed toward the chairs. We each took a seat.

"Now, sit back and get comfortable. They're La-Z Boys."

Murph and I reclined as instructed. There was something about this room that was familiar. I'm sure I came into it as a child, but it was something else. The vibe or aura of it was inviting making me less anxious and feeling in tune with myself, as I hadn't felt in a long time.

"I'm going to go through a guided meditation with you. You needn't do anything. You don't even have to concentrate on my words. All you need to do is relax and be open."

Fiona continued talking. I had the sensation that I was floating, that my mind was free from my body and that I could do anything, be anything and know everything. As she finished talking, I continued to drift to a wonderful place and I knew that what had happened to me was a blip and that soon it would be over. She brought us back to the room with a gentle urging.

"That was beautiful," I said.

"Everything is so clear," Murph added.

"Good. Let's celebrate. Out to the atrium for some champagne." She smiled and walked out of the room.

Murph took my hand, the beauty that surged through my body was overwhelming and a tear streamed down my face.

He looked at me with concern, "What's the matter? Don't cry, baby."

I looked into those beautiful eyes and said, "They're tears of joy. I get it. It's inside of me. I only have to quiet down and connect with my power and then I can see what I need to see. For years I didn't understand, but now I know."

He smiled, "Me too. Let's go get some champagne."

Fiona popped the cork and was pouring into the glasses. She turned to us handing each of us a glass. She picked up her glass raising it, "To family."

We raised ours. "Family," we said in unison.

"Questions?" Fiona asked.

"Only one," I said.

Fiona drew her lips tight anticipating the question she didn't want to answer.

"Where is my mother?"

Fiona took a long sip from her glass. She placed it down in front of her and looked me in the eye. "I have no idea. She left one day. There was a note. Actually two identical notes. One for me. One for your father."

"Can I see it?" I was hopeful that this would explain her disappearance and shed some light on why my father was so tight lipped about her departure.

"I burned it years ago." Fiona got up and walked about her plants, gathering dead leaves.

"Do you remember what it said?" I asked hoping for a resolution.

She sat back down. "Murph, could you give us a minute?"

"Of course," he said. He got up and walked outside.

"Is it that bad?" I asked.

She took a deep breath, "It said married and being a mother isn't all that it's cracked up to be. I'm leaving. Don't look for me."

I shook my head. I brought my hands up rubbing my temples. "Ouch. I think the knife that slashed my throat was gentler than that."

"Your mother was a free spirit. Very independent," Fiona's voice trailed off.

"Self-centered bitch, if you ask me," I answered.

"Don't let her actions harden your heart. She was always different. I thought it was a phase, maybe even postpartum depression, but then I realized I had to stop making excuses. She did what she did and there is no explanation other than that she wanted out."

"Thanks for telling me. It couldn't have been easy."

"It wasn't easy, especially for your father. He loved her so. I guess it wasn't enough. But now Tisha, you have your whole glorious life ahead of you. We'll get through this nightmare and move on. Forward, always look forward."

"Thanks. I was afraid to come to see you, but now that I did, I wish I had come sooner."

"Everything happens for a reason. It was time to come now."

"My head is spinning. I need to take this all in and then I need to figure out what I want to do with my life." I watched as Murph sat on the rocks looking out at the water. I wish I had a camera with me; it was the perfect photo op.

"What do you want to do?" she asked pouring herself another glass of champagne.

"Another?" Fiona waved the bottle in front of me.

"What the heck," I raised my glass for a pour. "I was talking to Bill about this. He thinks I should get back into my art, maybe open a gallery or do pop ups or a website."

"And what do you think?"

"I think it's going to take more money than I have."

"And if that wasn't an obstacle?"

"Maybe. I do love making things especially throwing clay and sculpting. But who would buy my stuff?"

"Get together a plan and we'll talk." She gave me a wink, looking outside she pointed toward Murph, "He's a wonderful man. You're very lucky."

"Yes, I am." Smiling we walked out to Murph to enjoy the seaside air.

CHAPTER 14

I didn't know if it was the champagne, the fresh air or the newfound answers to my questions, but I slept the entire drive back to Locust Valley. I felt a gentle shake and was greeted with a light kiss.

"Time to wake up sleepy head," Murph whispered in my ear.

"Home already?" I asked stretching my limbs.

"You looked so peaceful. It's been a long day. I guess I should be going."

"You guessed wrong. Come on upstairs," I said in my most sultry voice.

He threw the door opened, scooped me up in his arms and carried me up the stairs, both of us laughing along the way. I fumbled through my purse and opened the door. He set me down and we raced to the bedroom. Tossing his jacket on the chair, he took me in his arms and gave me the kiss I was yearning for all day. It started out slow and soft, but grew in intensity. He kissed my cheeks, my chin and made his way to my neck as we settled down on the bed. My body tingled with excitement and anticipation. I ran my hands through his lush hair, caressed his forearms and I began unbuttoning his shirt.

Commotion from outside startled us. Tires screeched. Shouting. A loud bang came from the garage. Murph jumped up stuffing his shirt into his pants and reached for his jacket pulling out his gun. "Call 911 and keep your head down," he shouted.

I grabbed my purse from under the covers of my duvet and pulled out my phone. I dialed and shouted into the phone, "Shots fired, shots fired. There are supposed to be police and security guarding me. Please come quickly." I gave the operator my address and hung up. I dialed my father. No answer. Getting up as much nerve as I could muster, I got out from the covers, crept to the window and peeked through. One of the security guards was lying face down in the driveway. Nothing else was visible. I wanted to look from another window, but I was afraid. Watching the beautiful gold clock next to my bed, the second hand moved at a snail's pace. It was almost as if it moved backward. The words of Nietzsche's famous quote resonated through my mind, *that which doesn't kill us makes us stronger*, but I didn't think so. It wears you down, wrings you out and tosses you to the ground like an unwanted piece of garbage. With every breath I took, my fear grew deeper, building until I thought I might burst like a balloon that happened upon a pin. I started to hyperventilate and was at a near panic when finally I heard the approaching sirens of the police. I dared to look out the window and found Murph waving his arms directing the police to the fallen security guard.

Throwing open the door, I bounded down the steps two at a time as an ambulance wailed into the driveway. The EMT's jumped from the vehicle to the aid of the downed man.

"What happened?" I screamed. "Where's Bill?" My eyes shot to Murph pleading for an answer.

Murph took me in his arms, "Calm down Tisha. He's not here. I don't know what happened."

"My dad, Beatrice. I tried to call, but they didn't answer." I was frantic. My mind was running in all different directions. I couldn't focus. I pulled my phone from my pocket and dialed Bill's cell number. I could hear Bill's ring tone from the garage. Hanging up, I dialed my father. He picked up on the third ring.

"Oh Dad get home, something's happened. Is Beatrice with you?"

"What's going on? Beatrice is with me. We're out shopping. We're just about finished. Calm down. What's the matter?"

"I don't know what's happening, but you need to get home. One of the guards was shot." I heard my father speaking to someone, but couldn't hear what he was saying.

"The security guard with us just got a call from base. We're on our way home. Are you okay?"

"I'm okay. Murph is here."

"What about your brother?"

I broke down sobbing. With all my might I said, "I don't know."

There was a flurry of police cars; ambulances, people running about and then questions flew at me. Everyone was talking at once. Their voices getting louder and louder. It was hard to understand what they were saying. I felt like a circuit whose capacity was being tested to see how much it could withstand before blowing. Lightheadedness enveloped me, morphing into dizziness, and then everything went black.

I woke up and was lying on my beautiful new sofa. Murph was sitting next to me with his head in his hands. I reached out to touch him. Was I dreaming? Did everything that I think just happened happen?

"Are you okay?" he asked and jumped up to be by my side.

"What happened? I remember people running around, cops, medics and the noise from downstairs. Please tell me what happened."

"Looks like someone ambushed your security guard. He was shot, but he's a retired cop and was wearing a vest. He'll be okay. Bad news, they took your brother."

"What do you mean *took* my brother?" I stood up with my fists clenched.

"He's been kidnaped. Your father let us look at the surveillance video. Two men ambushed the guard and then they took your brother. They were wearing masks so no ID yet. Looks like pros."

"But why? Why would they want my brother? Do you think it has something to do with the mob guys my uncle was involved with? Or with whatever the hell is going on with me? Oh God, no. It can't be my fault. He's my brother." I couldn't control my emotions. I fell down into a heap and sobbed.

Murph pulled me into his arms and held me.

"Could be but I don't think so. Whoever it was got past all of your brother's safeguards. Your uncle and his crew are not that sophisticated. Something else is happening here."

"What do we do?" I tried to collect myself. I needed to be strong, get myself together and think.

"Right now we wait. Your brother chose the security team. The head of the company is on his way over. Your father and I are going to sit down with him and see what we can come up with." I got up and walked into the bathroom. I turned the cold water on and splashed my face. Toweling myself dry, I looked into the mirror. Mirror, mirror, I'm going to get the bastard who took my brother. With my renewed strength and resolve, I marched back into the living room.

"Count me in. I'm sick and tired of sitting around like a victim, waiting for these fools to strike again. Now it's mine time to turn the tables. No one is fucking with my family."

BLINDSIGHT

BOOK 3

Susan Peterson Wisnewski

CHAPTER 1

There are few things in this world that infuriate me. Rude drivers, long lines, a coveted outfit not available in my size and lack of coffee in the morning are on the list. Screwing with my family tops it. My brother, Bill, had been kidnaped. I was pissed and needed to find out why he was taken.

The police questioned me, my father and Beatrice, my father's wife, over and over asking the same questions in different ways until I was ready to jump over the kitchen table and choke one of them. My grams, my father's mother, saved the day by arriving with two of her team of attorneys. Any further questioning would be done with them present. Murph, my boyfriend and suspended detective, was outside with a team of detectives, his coworkers, trying to piece together how the abduction happened. The Feds were on their way since there was a possible link between the murder of Mario DeVito, my bail jumping Uncle Chet, and the murder of TV journalist Barbara Gallant. This was all getting way to complicated and verging on pure crazy. However, it was happening and I needed for all of it to be solved or go away before I lost my sanity. Most of all, I needed my brother home, alive and well. He was my rock, best friend and confidant.

Everything was an effort. Breathing, talking, walking, thinking; I couldn't get out of my fog. I went up to my apartment to try and sleep. The dream was back. The damned, dark black nothingness dream that had come to haunt me whenever my life got rough was back again. Waking from my sleep attempt, I decided it was time for action. I was tired of feeling like a victim and even more tired of acting like one. Getting up, I decided to download the MP3 my grandmother gave me. My estranged grandmother, Fiona, was nothing at all like what I feared and built her up to be. I had stayed away because she brought up all kinds of questions I had about my mother who left when I was a young child. Somehow, I thought that by connecting with Fiona, I would learn the truth about my mother and I wouldn't like what I found out. What I did I learn was Fiona was as much in the dark about my mother as I, and sometimes there aren't answers and you need to let things go. She also told me that I needed to look more into myself so I could connect with a gift I have. I can touch a person's hand and see their past, present and future. This gift, or curse, scares me but it's time I meet it head on. Fiona is a medium, herbalist and all around interesting woman. Our recent attempt at reconnecting left me hopeful that I would straighten out my life and pursue my dreams getting back on a track to doing instead of whining.

Pulling my iPad out of a drawer, I added the download to my iTunes list. Sitting back in a comfortable chair, I closed my eyes and listened to the gentle, lyrical words in Fiona's voice. It was a revelation. Her convincing words assured me that I would connect, could connect, with my gift and move forward. I opened my eyes and before me stood Barbara and Mario.

"Hi," I said.

"Any progress?" Barbara asked. She glided around the room looking at the furniture, eyeing the Jura espresso machine and finally sat down on the sofa.

Mario was much milkier than the previous visits. Rather than the vivid view of a real life person, blood soaked gut and all, he was filmy. Barbara was still her beautiful self even with the gapping chest hole where the high-powered rifle robbed her of life.

"Nothing yet and now my brother has been kidnaped," I said.

"Hmmm, your brother works for that company down in Pittsburgh. A so called think tank, but I found out it is funded by not only the Company, but a few other rather questionable interests."

"What do you mean?"

"The writing's on the wall. Your brother creates all types of tracking and surveillance devices. His company sells them to the highest bidder. This is high stakes stuff, honey. You need to put it all together," Barbara said sitting back in the chair and playing with her long blonde hair.

"But how? I don't know what he does other than create those crazy robots and other technical stuff. He must be good. He makes a ton of money. Are you implying he's doing something illegal?"

"Maybe not illegal. Ethics are what I had in mind. Think about the entire picture, there's something you're not seeing."

"But why can't you clue me in. You're the one that's dead; you were on to something before you were shot. What was it?" I got up and looked out the window because I thought I heard something outside. I saw one of the security guards checking something out as he walked around the driveway.

"Just because I'm dead doesn't make me a see all, know all. It doesn't work like that."

"How does it work?"

"I have no idea. I'm new to this. I still know what I was working on. Not much more. There is a link between your uncle, Mario and your brother's company, but that's as far I as got. I figured if I could befriend you, I would be able to get closer to Bill and perhaps get some insider info."

"Thanks for the vote of confidence. I thought you were a shoulder to cry on."

"Look at where it got me." Barbara got up and pointed to her wound.

"Oh yeah, sorry about that."

"It's not so bad, I'm starting to adjust. I do need answers. Answers, so I can finish my journey. I don't want to be hovering forever."

Mario was fading into the background, becoming dimmer and dimmer. I pointed his way.

"What's with him?" I asked.

"He's transitioning. He still won't talk about who killed him and it's starting to bug me, but up here, or in between I should say, there isn't anything I can use to get him to talk, so it's his decision if he'll spill or not."

"I can't believe I'm sitting here talking to ghosts."

"At least you aren't one. And I prefer spirit. Ghost is too icky," Barbara said squinting her nose.

"I'd like to keep it that way." I rubbed my eyes trying to make heads or tails of what she had told me.

Barbara and Mario faded and as quickly as they came, they were gone. I needed to find the connection and now I thought I knew where to start. Peeking out of my window, I saw the coast was clear. I made my way downstairs to the garage and let myself in. The Feds confiscated Bill's laptop, but I knew where he hid a copy of his backups. Opening the double doors of the closet that held my pottery collection I reached into an opalescent vase that was shoved in a corner in the back. Digging down into it, I picked out a USB drive. Placing it in my pocket, I closed the doors. Peering out of the window of the door, I saw that again the coast was clear and scrambled up the steps to see what Bill had been working on.

Getting comfortable at the kitchen table, I remembered something that Bill had told me about covering all of my bases. Before I opened my laptop, I turned off my router and pulled the power cord from the wall. For an added measure of security, I walked around the apartment drawing the curtains on all of the windows. Settling back down, I placed the key drive into my laptop and tried to open its contents. There was a password. I tried simple ones. I tried less simple ones. I smacked my laptop. Nothing. I needed to get that password.

Head in my hands, I rubbed my forehead. Bill was a computer wiz. He probably used some crazy random numbers that was some sort of equation for a math problem he solved. And then it clicked. We had a conversation a few weeks before about my life. Not actually my life, but my stalled life and how I wasn't using my creative talents and hiding behind things that were easy. I didn't need a password. All through school, I made it my hobby to bypass passwords to get into places I had no business being in, like teacher's accounts and upcoming exams. I never used anything I found to cheat, but the excitement of the challenge was like a drug. When I was found out there was hell to pay. Well not hell, suspension and the promise I'd never do it again.

It was time to get my brain in tune and carry on with my prior delinquent behavior. It's quite simple if you know what to do. Rather than going through the infinite possibilities of password combinations, I copied the thumb drive to another drive. Getting into the C drive, I replicated the data. Getting back into the data, it prompted me for a new user and password on the replication. It was a little more involved than that, but a girl's got to have some secrets. The important thing was it worked. I was in.

CHAPTER 2

A s the files were loading onto my laptop, a picture of Bill appeared. He was smiling. A mischievous smile. As if one of my ghosts, make that spirits, were coming to me. A hazy version of Bill rose from my laptop. I fell backward almost knocking the chair out from beneath me.

"What the fuck?"

"Relax, Tisha. It's not me, only a hologram of me. If you've gotten this far, I'm proud of you. You're using your brain again. I know it's you because I have few safeguards installed. First, this hologram will only work on your computer. I took the liberty of installing recognition software on your laptop. Next, I also installed a retina ID sequence. So as they say in *Mission Impossible*, this USB will self-destruct if you're not Tisha looking back at me."

"You're impossible," I said to the hovering apparition.

"To begin, it is imperative that you contact Sam Jones at the Acme Security Company. His company is providing the security team for the house. Don't blame them for whatever has happened to me. There are forces out there that will do anything to get their hands on a new technology I've been developing. You can trust Sam. He's the best at what he does. Give him this flash drive after you finish watching this. There are codes and information that he will need to help find me. Be careful. He has an office in Locust Valley, but let him come to you so it will look less obvious since it's on him that I'm missing. I'm still not sure where all the pieces of this fit together, but I think it all leads back to Uncle Chet. So far, every time I start to make some headway, his name pops up. He's involved up to his ears. I don't understand how, but the why is almost sure to be money. Hopefully, this will all be over soon. Love you, sis. Be strong. I'll see you soon."

His image faded into nothingness. My resolve morphed into all-consuming focus.

As I was about to find the number for the Acme Security Company, wondering why he would name a company after something out of the *Road Runner*, I heard a knock at my door. I pushed aside the curtain to find my father accompanied by a hulk of a man. I opened the door.

"Hi Dad," I said opening the door to let him and his companion in.

He kissed my cheek. "Hi Tisha. How are you holding up? This is Sam Jones, the owner of the security company. He would like to ask you a few questions."

Sam Jones was a mountain of a man. His must have been at least six five, with arms cut to perfection. His chiseled chest strained against a black tee shirt in a very pleasing way. He had incredible eyes. Obsidian would be the best way to describe them. The darkest eyes I had ever seen. Dark in a soulful way.

"Can I get you some coffee? Espresso? Cappuccino?" I asked as I made my way over to make myself an espresso.

"I'm good," my father said.

"If it's not too much trouble, an espresso would be great," Sam said in a matter of fact way.

I pressed the buttons on my fancy new machine and produced two perfect cups. My father and Sam sat down in the living room. Sam draped his leather jacket over the back of one of the kitchen chairs. I handed Sam his coffee and took a seat across from them on the sofa. I needed to get rid of my father so I could explain to Sam about the flash drive, but the how eluded me.

"Tisha, could you tell me exactly what happened from the time you left your grandmother's house to the time you heard the commotion from downstairs." It was the perfect opening.

"Dad, I hope you don't mind, but some of the things I said to Fiona are personal."

My father rose. "I understand completely, honey. If you need me I'll be at the house." It wasn't all true, but it achieved my purpose.

"Thanks, Dad." I watched as he walked out of the apartment. Turning to Sam, I said, "I didn't want him to hear what I'm going to say." I pulled the flash drive from my pocket and handed it to him adding, "Bill made this drive. I'm guessing in the last few days. He told me that all the poking around he's been doing leads to my Uncle Chet. He also said that there is information on the drive that will help you find him."

"Fantastic. Now, if we could go over the events of today," he leaned back and gazed at me, waiting for me to begin.

"There's not much to tell. Murph and I were driven out to my maternal grandmother's house by Marco. Curtis came too and sat in the front seat of the car. When we arrived, Curtis took a look around the house and told us it was okay to get out of the car. We had a conversation with my grandmother about a talent I have, and she was able to shed some light on it. That was about all. Oh no wait, my grandmother told me that Beatrice called her to tell her we were on our way to visit, but I never said a word to Beatrice about the trip. Murph took apart my cell phone and pulled out a tiny disk. He said it was a bug. He crushed it on some rocks and found a bottle on the beach and threw it into the Long Island Sound."

Sam's expression gave away nothing.

"We had some lunch. My grandmother guided us through a meditation and then we left. I slept on the way home. Murph and I came upstairs. The next thing I know, I heard tires screeching, shouting and a loud boom. Murph jumped up, got his gun, told me to call 911 and ran down the stairs."

"Tell me more about the conversation between Beatrice and your grandmother." He looked straight in my eye when he spoke, his gaze unnerving me.

"It was simply that she called. I didn't question my grandmother about it."

"Are the two close?"

"No. In fact that's what was so odd about it. Fiona and my family have been estranged. My mother left when I was very young and in some ways my father blamed my grandmother for my mother's departure."

"Okay. Can I have her address? I'd like to talk to her."

"Sure," I pulled out my phone and showed him her entry.

"Tell me more about Murph. When did you meet him?" This was getting uncomfortable. Why did he want to know more about Murph?

"He's the detective on a case I witnessed," I started.

He put up his massive hand to stop me. He listened for a moment. Getting up, he moved toward the front door. His ease and grace was unusual for a man of his size. The door flew open and Beatrice was standing on the other side.

"Goodness, ya'll scared the life out of me. With all this craziness, I thought I'd bring ya'll a little bit to eat. We need to keep up our strength."

"Beatrice, I appreciate it, but I'm not in the mood to eat right now." Her face dropped.

I continued, "Well, maybe later. Thanks." I took the tray from her and closed the door before she had a chance to say another word. I could hear her stepping back down the stairs and drew back the curtain to be sure she was gone.

Sam got up and went toward the kitchen area. He opened a few cabinets, found a plate and took it out. He removed the contents of the platter onto the plate. Turning the platter over, he examined it. He picked his jacket up from the chair, pulling out what appeared to be a flat iron. He waved the device over the platter. It remained silent. He continued waving the equipment throughout my space. The apartment was bug free.

"Wanted to be sure there weren't any other uninvited guests," Sam said chuckling, "Tell me about Beatrice," he said sitting back down.

"I know less about her than my grandmother. She appeared about six months ago and the next thing I knew, they eloped. She's from down south somewhere and she has a half dozen cats. I'm allergic to cats. Very allergic. I'm having a hard time warming up to her."

"Okay. Back to Murph," he said shifting in his seat and crossing his legs.

"He was assigned to the case with the murder I witnessed. We talked a few times about the case, but it wasn't going anywhere. He called me on my way into work and told me not to go to in. You know the rest."

"Why did he want to meet you?"

I started squirming. I didn't want to get Murph in any trouble. "This stays between us, right?"

"I work for your family. Your brother and I have been working together on some joint ventures for a few years. This is all about your family."

"Okay. He had been tipped off by a Federal agent he's friendly with that there was going to be a raid on Uncle Chet's office. He didn't want me to get caught up in the shuffle."

"But, you were almost killed," Sam pointed out.

"Yeah, but he saved me. He shot that Brickyard Mike guy before he could kill me." I didn't like what he was implying.

"Tisha, it's my job to look at everything from an impartial viewpoint. Some questions may be difficult, but in order to get your brother back, I need to see the whole picture." He flashed a smile that could melt a glacier.

He had me. "Okay. What do we do now?" I sat crossing and uncrossing my legs.

"Now, I go back to my office and take a look at this thumb drive. Then my team and I will get all of our facts together and go from there."

"Do you think Murph had anything to do with this?" My stomach was in knots.

"I don't know what to think right now. There are a few leads we were getting close to getting answers on, but now with the abduction, it might shed some light on some of the questions we had and point us in the right direction."

"How can I help?"

He grinned as he rose, inches from me. "You can help by staying here in your apartment. If you need anything, have one of my men go with you, or better yet, have them get it for you. The next two days are critical."

"What about the bug thing? If it is Murph, what should I do?" It couldn't be Murph. He was my savior. When I touched his hand it was beauty and fireworks, not an inkling of bad vibes.

"Keep an eye on him. Or better yet, tell him you have a headache," he grinned again.

Unable to control myself, I gave him a jab, "Who is it that's been listening in?"

"Not me, cross my heart," Sam laughed.

"Just what I need, another impossible smart ass. Go. I promise to be careful and hole up in my now stunning apartment."

"It is very nice."

"I have Beatrice to thank for that." I scanned the room. She outdid herself surprising me on my return from the hospital by creating my dream apartment.

"Keep your eyes peeled and call me if you need me. Anytime. Day or night." Sam picked up my phone and plugged his number into it.

"Will do," I said. I watched as he walked out the door. What a butt.

CHAPTER 3

I tried to watch some inane TV but it wasn't working. Flipping from channel to channel, nothing kept my attention. Looking at the plate of snacks Beatrice brought up earlier, I tipped the chicken wings and ribs into the trash. Searching the fridge for something to eat, I pulled out a wheel of goat cheese Brie and a Fuji apple leaving them out on the counter to warm to room temperature. I almost wished for my boring, pathetic, nothing life back, but instead looked on the bright side. I had reconciled with Fiona, learned about my gift and a way to channel it and I met Murph.

I didn't agree with Sam. There was no way Murph was involved with Bill's abduction. To be sure, I would watch what I said and be cautious for now, but knew it wasn't necessary.

I needed to do something to get my mind off of my situation, to help. Pulling out a sketchpad, I decided to try my hand at diagraming the situation. I made a bunch of circles. First, there was my Uncle Chet and Brickyard Mike. Then there was Mario DeVito, Brickyard Mike and maybe Kevin O'Sullivan. Next were Barbra Gallant and her killer. And finally, my brother. The one common factor was my uncle.

Beatrice had to be somewhere or somehow involved. What did I know about her? I wanted to look up her info, but before I did, I needed secure lines. I turned my router back on and typed in a sequence to reroute my search. If anyone tried to trace where the inquiries were coming from, they would find a host of servers, IP addresses and various countries around the world all going in a long convoluted circle. They would never find the search was coming from me. I typed her name. I wasn't sure if she had a middle name so I typed Beatrice Allen. Nothing came up. Then I typed Beatrice Allen, Alabama. Still nothing. Maybe it was Mississippi. Again nothing. I was getting frustrated. I knew I shouldn't perform the next search, but I couldn't help myself. I rerouted again and searched wedding records. Yes, I was accessing county records and I got into files that were supposed to be confidential, but extreme circumstances calls for extreme measures. Their wedding application popped up and gave me a social security number. I rerouted once again. This time I searched her social security numbers and found out exactly what I thought I would. The number she provided didn't register. The number was bad.

I took another look in a select few areas and there had been activity beginning six months prior to the time she had been married to my father. It would typically take about a year before any flags would be raised, but as she wasn't applying for credit or using the number for employment, it could take years.

Beatrice wasn't Beatrice. No surprise there. Now, what would I do with the information?

Another reroute and I tried Uncle Chet. Chester James Adams. The search brought dozens upon dozens of files. I categorized them according to subject. I need to understand what he was doing, what he was accused of doing and how this mess all added up to an attempt on my life and the abduction of my brother. I had a long night of reading ahead of me.

A knock on the door distracted me. I brought my laptop into the bedroom and tossed a sweatshirt over it. Making my way back to the door, I glanced at the clock over my kitchen sink, it read ten pm.

Murph was standing at the door with a big smile on his handsome face, his eyes revealing the torment of the day and a need for rest.

"Come in," I said, pulling him toward me.

"Just for a minute. I have my hearing tomorrow morning. I wanted to be sure you're okay before I went home," he said reaching over to meet my embrace.

"I'm okay. What do your fellow police think about all of this?"

"There are so many unknowns. Whoever took your brother is a pro. They were in and out in seconds. Somehow, they got through the security gate without a hitch, tackled Johnson and grabbed your brother. Twenty, twenty-two seconds tops."

"What about the car? Did you see the license plates?"

"No, there weren't any. It was a black Cadillac Escalade SUV. Thousands of them are registered in the metro area. Their expertise signals pros so that eliminates a bunch of possible suspects."

"So now what?" I released him and walked into the living area.

"We wait and see what the hell is going on." He let out a big yawn. "Sorry about that. I'm going to get going. I have a big day tomorrow and I need some sleep."

"What's going to happen to you?"

"I'm not sure. I've never been to one of these before. I'm new to the force. I got pushed up to detective because I kept my mouth shut about something I saw that would have embarrassed one of my superiors. Took the test like he told me to and *bam*, detective. I need to think about a lot of things." He looked off past me and at the ceiling as if one of the cracks would be a portal of knowledge.

"What do you mean?" I didn't understand where he was going.

"Don't worry. Once it's over, I'll give you a call and we can talk. Wish me luck." He gave me a quick kiss and headed for the door.

"What time is it scheduled for?" I asked as I followed him out.

"Eleven," he answered turning back toward me.

"Okay, well good luck or break a leg. Do you want me to come with you?"

"Not a good idea. One of the first questions they're going to ask is why I called you. I think it would be better if you weren't anywhere near that hearing."

"I guess you're right." I gave him a squeeze and looked up at him. Our lips met. The magic, the fire, the chemistry shook the ground. There was no way he had anything to do with what happened.

CHAPTER 4

Watching Murph walk to his car, I wondered what was bothering him. I was sure the hearing had him on edge, but there was something else going on that he wasn't sharing with me.

Getting back to research, I started taking notes. Uncle Chet was something else. He'd been arrested a few times for petty crimes but never convicted and most of the time, charges were dropped. From the arrests records, it appeared he was working with the Mafia as well as the newer Russian syndicate. That would explain his connection to Brickyard Mike, Mario DeVito, Kevin O'Sullivan and the gorillas he had patting down visitors at the door of his office. The Russian connection I didn't understand yet.

As long as there was money to be made, Uncle Chet tried to have a hand in it. At one point he sold commercial insurance. He had his license revoked when he was caught collecting premiums but not bothering with the mundane task of buying insurance policies with the money. He paid a fine and restitution to his victims, or it looks like Grams paid, and off he went to find his next scam. I needed to talk to my paternal grandmother about this debacle.

Next was his involvement with the Mafia. He had been hauled in during a sting operation in Brooklyn. He was part of a group lending money at astronomical rates. He was charged with loansharking. The charges were dropped.

Next, he was accused of being a bookie and involved with sports gambling. That explained all of the TV's in his office. How could I be so stupid? I guess I never expected my uncle to be involved with anything really illegal. The people coming and going from the office were paying or getting money. I wonder if the delivery I made to the city was a payment. This was getting too weird. My dad was the ultimate all American good boy, my grandmother the quintessential Locust Valley lockjaw. I never met my grandfather; he passed away long before I was born. His name graced more than a few buildings in Manhattan as well as a number of foundations all on the up and up. From what my father said, it was his grandfather, my great grandfather who was a captain of industry. He started in banking and then grew his empire adding oil and real estate to the mix. He was a wheeler-dealer at a time made ripe for the enterprising young man. His efforts afforded our family our lush home as well as healthy trust accounts. My grandfather continued in his father's footsteps, but his life was cut short at an early age from a heart attack. My grandmother continued the family business, although Grams sold off most of the real estate and oil operations, she chose to focus on overseeing investment portfolios.

The question that hung unanswered was why did my uncle choose his lifestyle when there was, from what I could see, more than enough money to go around? Or was it the blue blood grandchild syndrome where the family money is squandered away by lazy, privileged grandchildren unable to find meaningful employment and having the lack of restraint needed to sustain a fortune? Again, my grandmother would have the answers or at least some clue as to why he chose the path he took. Rather than speculate, I would go to Grams in the morning. It was past three am. I needed sleep.

As I lay in bed waiting for sleep to take me, I thought about the information I accumulated. The connection to the crimes I witnessed and my uncle's petty crimes weren't adding up. Why the murders? Why the kidnapping? What was the reason? And how did Beatrice fit into the puzzle, if she was even involved? Information overload took over. I got up, drank a glass of water, went to the bathroom washed my face and dabbed some lavender oil on my wrists and neck. The sweet aroma relaxed me. Back to bed, I fell asleep in no time.

Sunlight streamed in through the pale blue velvet curtains that adorned my windows. Rolling over and sneaking a peek at my clock with one eye, my brain processed it was nine am. Wanting to rollover and go back to sleep, I thought about something my uncle said to me. Before I went on my last errand for him in the city he said that I was like him. I didn't know what he meant. Perhaps he was referring to the way I won't stop at anything when I have my mind set on something. He was right. Maybe I did cut corners and do some things that were marginally questionable, but I did it to help people, not for greed. There was a huge difference between us. I knew my family had money. Having my family bail me out of messes well into my forties wasn't something I would do. I would find my place in life soon. I just had to. I got up and jumped into the shower. Sleep would wait.

Dressing in a pair of navy blue capris, a white blouse and black ballet flats I made my way down the steps to be greeted by this morning's security guard. He had a gun. Not a simple handgun, but a big machine gun strapped over his shoulder. This was too real.

"Morning," I called to him.

"Morning. Lovely day. May I ask where you're going?" he asked.

The day was a stunner. Blue sky, birds singing, spring awakening in full force and a man armed with a machine gun wanting to know where I was going. Surreal.

"To visit my grandmother in her cottage," I answered.

"Okay. I'll walk with you." He spoke into his shoulder, "Miss T enroute to Mrs. A. Copy?"

Blipping sounds emerged from his shoulder. "Copy," his shoulder replied.

We strolled the short walk, passing the back of the house and pool, beyond the stables and down a path to her front door where another guard sat, also armed. Ringing the bell, I stepped back and nodded to my guards. I wanted to tell them how much I appreciated what they were doing, but I thought it would sound trite. When this was all over, I would find a way to thank them.

The door opened revealing my grandmother in her usual impeccable dress. As children, Bill and I would joke that Grams didn't sleep, but would plug herself into an outlet at night and recharge for the next day all dressed in her prim and proper suits, sensible heels, coiffed hair and strand of pearls. No matter what time we arrived, she was dressed and ready for us. It must have taken a toll on her to be thrust into taking charge of two young children. I was three and my brother had just turned two when my mother left. My grandmother came to the rescue, moving into the main house and taking over the day-to-day responsibilities of raising a family. I know my father was a mess. I remember his lying in bed for days and days not wanting to have anything to do with the world. Grams saw him and us through it all. Her business obligations were moved to the house and she wouldn't think twice of conducting a meeting with the two of us scampering about. Our robust behavior seemed to delight her even though her own sensibilities leaned toward restraint and candor.

"Tisha dear, come in," Grams said.

I walked into her cottage. It had been some time since I was in this grand place. She moved into the city when Bill and I went off to college preferring New York to Long Island. She made it out for all of the family functions and would return to the city after the events were over. She loved art, and nothing compared to the city and its museums. Quite the collection was evident from the representation on her walls. She preferred abstract expressionist work with a de Kooning gracing the large living room wall. Next to his painting were two of mine when I tried my hand at his style. I smiled remembering what she said to me when I presented them to her. She said that I could be anything and do anything that I put my heart to. My renditions, clearly amateur, did have an attitude about them. Connecting with that part of me became goal number two.

"Morning Grams. You're looking well," I said kissing her cheek.

"As are you. How are you holding up?" She pointed toward the kitchen.

I walked over to the counter and helped myself to a cup of coffee.

"May I pour for you?" I asked.

"Please. And there are some croissants in the fridge. Be a dear and pop them in the oven for a minute. There should be some jam too." She made her way to the kitchen table sitting down and looking out the French doors to the garden. "Lovely day today. The garden is looking beautiful. That is the one thing I miss living in the city."

"It is beautiful. Maybe, I'll start a vegetable garden like we did when I was a kid. I could grow some lettuce and greens. Maybe a few tomatoes." I could tell she wasn't listening. I took two dainty cups from the cupboard and poured the coffee. I filled the matching pitcher with cream. Placing a couple of croissants in the oven, I set the timer for five minutes and brought the coffee to the table.

"You're somewhere else," I said sitting down. It was easy not to pay attention with the view from outside.

"I'm sick about Bill. I don't want to think about what's happened, let alone what might happen. The police or these security people must find him. It will kill me if anything bad happens to him." She hung her head and cried. I wrapped my arms around her trying to console her. She took a deep breath. "Enough of the weakness. I'm going to call a few people and see if they can help." A newfound resolve washed away her tears.

"Grams, I've been doing some digging."

She gave me a *what are you getting in the middle of* kind of look. "What kind of digging are you talking about?" she asked.

"I got on my computer and tried to make some sense of everything. Grams, I know I swore I would never put my nose where it didn't belong again, but there is too much at stake. I hacked a bunch of sites."

"Your father worked very hard to send you to the best schools and this is how you repay him?" She got up and paced around the kitchen. "Well, don't keep me in knots. What did you find out?"

The ready bell sounded. Grams removed the croissants from the oven, placed one on each plate, brought them over to the table and took her seat.

"There was a lot of information about Uncle Chester. His arrests and bailouts." I took a bite of the flaky pastry. It melted in my mouth, the luscious butter-packed treat tasted sublime. Daring to look at my Grams, I could see her lips were pursed and she was wondering where to begin.

"Your uncle had always been different. I joked with your grandfather that he must have been switched at birth. He believed that the nurse dropped him on his head several times as there was no doubt he was an Adams. He was a handsome boy in his younger years resembling his grandfather. As he grew older, I suspect he dabbled in drugs. He looks old for his age. No matter how much discipline we tried to instill, he was always getting into mischief. His mischief turned to petty theft. It was as if he found more pleasure in trying to cheat someone than working for whatever it was that he wanted. Your father was the complete opposite. He is a gentle, studious soul, always kind and would never even look at someone in an unkind way no less cheat them. I spent years bailing your uncle out as petty theft turned to outright stealing. I failed him somehow. It has been the guilt that made me feel compelled to bail him out and pay for his sins. And pay I did. Victims, insurance companies, lawyers, bail bondsmen ... the list was endless. About nine months ago, I sat him down and told him it was over. He expended his trust fund and his inheritance. He would not get a penny more from me nor would I bail him out again. Of course, I did bail him out again and now he's on the loose." She looked out into the garden, lost in her thoughts.

"Nine months ago. Hmm. What do you know about Beatrice?"

"Not much. What are you getting at?" She was scanning her memory trying to make a connection. She pushed her plate away and drank the last bit of her coffee.

"I did a search on her, but couldn't come up with anything."

"Well, dear, maybe she's not a criminal."

"I mean nothing. Nothing for her name, social security number. Nothing. Her name and number appeared a little less than a year ago, nothing before that."

Raising her eyebrows, she said, "At least she signed a prenuptial. I insisted the lawyers draw one up when your father called to tell me he was eloping. Did you confront her?"

"No, like I said, I found out last night. After I speak with you, I was going to talk with Sam Jones from the security company to see if he can find out more about her."

Grams got up and picked up her phone. She began to dial a number. I raced over to her and took the phone from her hand, signaling her to be quiet. I opened the battery area and checked for a disk.

"No need to do that. Security inspected the house this morning."

"But what about the way they were able to trace calls from landlines outside of the house? I have my cell. It's clean. You can make your call from it."

Handing her the phone, she dialed and started to talk, "I need for you to find out some information about someone. Yes. Everything. Beatrice Allen," she held her hand over the phone and looked to me, "Do you know her birthday?"

"I think March. The beginning. Dad had a little party for her. She wouldn't tell us how old she is. Do you want me to look up her wedding records again?"

"No dear. Let these gentlemen handle it." She turned her attention back to the phone. "Sometime in March, but it could be a fake. Okay. Let me know if you need anything else." She handed me back my phone.

We sat back down at the table. She began drumming her fingers on the damask tablecloth. I started to get up when the phone rang. The number wasn't familiar save the 212 area code: New York City.

"Were you expecting a call back?"

She gave me a smile and took the phone from me. "Hello. Yes. I knew you gentlemen are on your toes. Let me get a piece of paper," she motioned toward a drawer. I pulled it open and removed a pad and pencil and brought them to her.

Listening to the man on the other end of the line, she started writing. I peered over her shoulder, watching as the words formed in her elegant cursive. Elizabeth Anthony, waitress, Elmhurst, 36, DOB 3/04/78, no warrants, some petty crime, shoplifting, bad checks, no sign of current employment.

"Thank you. Yes, if I need anything else, I'll be sure to," she hung up and gave me a sly grin.

"Grandmother, you've been holding out on me."

"Do you expect that I wouldn't question a new member of the family? I had my attorneys check her out. I didn't want to be bothered with any details unless they were material. There was a file created and as you can see from my list, not much other than poor judgment. If you were brought this information, what would you think?"

I took another glance at the list. "I'd think that it was a woman getting on in years that made some bad choices. Wait a minute, 1978 that makes her 36, she still looks okay but knew she was running out of time. She met a man and turned on her charms."

"Good girl. My attorneys monitor everything. There have been no outlandish withdrawals from any of the accounts, there is a prenuptial so your father's trust money is safe, and other than her name situation there hasn't been anything to raise a red flag."

"Okay, but she did lie." I didn't like this. I got up. "He should know that's she's been lying to him."

"Tisha, your loyalty to your father is commendable, but sit down for a minute and listen to what I have to say."

I knew she was about to convince me of something I didn't want to be convinced about. The truth was, I didn't like Beatrice or Elizabeth or Betty or whoever she was. Her stupid southern bullshit drawl was ... bullshit. The damn cats that crept through the house like sinister demons making it off limits to me, pissed me off. My father had a right to know she was a fraud.

"When your mother left your father it came close to killing him. It took years for him to put it behind him. He never got over it and probably never will. He hasn't dated or had the company of a woman in almost twenty years. He turned all of his efforts to his work and to you and Bill. With the two of you going out on your own, I was afraid for him. Afraid he'd fall back into that horrible depression that almost took him away from us. He met this woman and she made herself into a persona to appeal to him. What harm is there in that? He's happy. I have an eye on things. If she has ulterior motives, I'll be the first to know." She gave me a challenging look.

"He is happy. I'll give you that. But keep both eyes on her."

She smiled, "They already are."

"Well, I'll let you get back to what you were doing. If it's okay, I'll share this bit about Beatrice with Sam." I gave her a kiss on the forehead.

"Sure, it will save him some legwork."

Leaving the house, I was met with my keeper of the day. I looked up at the sky. Nothing bad could happen on a day as glorious as this. I turned to him and said, "Can you get hold of Sam? I need to talk to him."

"Of course," he led me back to my stairway and as I ascended, I heard him place the call to Sam. Yes, today was going to be a very good day.

CHAPTER 5

Stretching out on my sofa, I thought about my conversation with my grandmother. She had a point about Beatrice and my father. No good would come from revealing Beatrice's deception unless it was necessary and became apparent her motives were less than honorable. I agreed with her choice to be quiet, but it didn't mean I had to like it. When I spoke with Murph after his hearing, I would see if he could find out anything about Beatrice and her newfound name.

My nerves kicked in, my hands started shaking when I thought about the hearing; it was almost twelve-thirty. I hoped it was going well. I wondered what he meant when he said he wasn't cut out to be a cop. What did he really want to do? My stomach growled. Pulling open the fridge, nothing enticed me. The cupboards, although full, were uninteresting. What did I want? I opened junk a drawer that held takeout menus. Pizza, sushi, Chinese, or Mexican food? Yes, cheese quesadillas from Cantina Bay in Bayville would be perfect. As I looked for my phone, I heard a knock. Sam was at the door.

"Come in."

"Hi. How are you holding up?" His gaze met mine. I looked away.

"Okay, I guess. I was going to order some takeout. Interested?" I walked toward the sofa.

"What did you have in mind?" He followed, sitting down.

"Mexican, a little spot in Bayville makes some great stuff. Their burritos, quesadillas, or if you want Italian, they also make great pasta, chicken and meatball dishes."

"Mexican Italian food," he laughed, "only in New York. I am starving, put me down for a burrito grandé deluxe and nachos grandé. Mind if I bring this down to the guys? It's all on me."

"Sure." I found a pad and pen handing them and the menu to him.

He went back out leaving the door open and returned a moment later.

"You wanted to see me?" he prompted.

"Yes, I was doing a little research." I reached back into my junk drawer and picked out a ponytail holder. Pulling my hair in it and away from my face, I turned back to him.

"Looks like Uncle Chet's been involved in all sorts of illegal activities."

"Yes, I know."

"And Beatrice Allen, isn't Beatrice Allen. Her name is Elizabeth Anthony. Her date of birth is 3/04/78 and she has an arrest record from some years back for shoplifting and cashing bad checks. She was working as a waitress up until about ten months ago when she sailed into my father's life and convinced her to marry him."

"How did you get all of that? We had been coming up blank."

"My grandmother."

He laughed. "It figures. I had a feeling she was in charge and wasn't giving us all the info available to her."

"She wants to spare my father any grief. She doesn't think there's any harm in her fibs as long as it was simply to catch herself a man. She doesn't want to tell my dad unless there is no other choice. Does anything you're working on connect? Do you know where Bill is or who has him?"

"Not yet, but I did uncover something."

A knock on the door shattered my attention. Sam answered it and took the food order. He said to the guard, "Send Jack to Cantina Bay in about fifteen." He pulled some money from his pocket handing it to him and closed the door.

"What did you find out?" I felt like I was traveling through a field covered in booby-traps. If I made the wrong move, I would fall into an abyss.

"It looks like our friend Murph has some explaining to do."

I folded my arms across my chest, my voice rose a few octaves, "What do you mean?"

"There was a forty thousand dollar deposit made into his bank account four months ago and another twenty-five yesterday. Plus he's been buying huge amounts of aluminum wire."

My mouth dropped. "Well maybe he got a raise or some windfall. And maybe he needs to rewire his house." I couldn't believe what I was hearing. Where would he get money like that?

"Detectives don't get raises like that. His family is middle class. Everyone has been on the job. Houses aren't wired with aluminum."

"But he saved me. He shot Brickyard Mike when he tried to kill me." I pleaded for him to listen, to change his mind and look in another direction.

"Think about it for a minute. He lured you to him when he asked you to meet him in the city. Why would anyone drop everything to meet someone they barely knew before work? How did Brickyard know you were on that train? How did he know about the raid? He's a Nassau detective not a Fed. Who would know that you're impulsive?"

"He said he has a friend who works for the Feds that tipped him off."

"It's unlikely. Those operations are kept top secret and can take years to put together. No one would want to jeopardize all of the time put into that kind of investigation."

"Well what about Barbara? No one knew we were meeting at the arboretum. Explain that."

"Wasn't it him who pulled out the bug in your phone and disposed of it without showing it to anyone?"

As much as I didn't want to believe him, these awful words made sense. I sunk down in my chair wanting to disappear into that abyss and for it to all go away. How could my power not see through Murph? Everything was beautiful when I touched him, unless my gift was gone. Maybe the shock of the knifing rendered me useless in the ways of seeing.

A knock on the door and the scent of Mexican food met us.

"Why don't we sit outside?" I suggested, "It's too beautiful a day to be indoors."

I brought out a handful of water bottles and a package of napkins and led him to the patio set on the deck overlooking the pool. Four more guards joined us. We ate in silence savoring the tasty morsels before us. The mood should have been animated given the beautiful day, but we were all on edge as I suspected the team had been briefed on Murph's possible involvement. Finishing my lunch, I cleared my plate, asked the men if they wanted anything else and retreated to my space. I sat grasping my pillow holding back the tears in a fetal position. Murph did have some serious explaining to do.

CHAPTER 6

G etting claustrophobic, I needed to clear my mind and get out of the house. I took a walk around the property. It wasn't the run or bike ride my body was craving, but the sun on my face and the feel of a cool breeze to perk me up. I sat by the pond watching a few of the goldfish swimming around after their long winter slumber. It was hard to comprehend how they shut down their bodies for months on end, floating near the bottom, not eating or moving around until the weather warmed. I wanted to summon Barbara and Mario to ask more questions, but I decided to wait until after my confrontation with Murph. I searched around for my fairy friends to appear for a sign from them that everything would be okay. They didn't appear; too many curious eyes wearing bulletproof vests were about. The sound of the gates opening took me out of my trance. I could see Murph's Mustang rounding the corner and parking in front of the garage. Sam stood in front of one of the bays waiting for him.

Picking up my pace, I called out, "Hey, Murph, over here," waving my arms wanting to be the one to ask the questions.

Sam joined him in coming over to me.

Murph was smiling, his gait relaxed. I hoped it was a good sign.

The two joined me, Murph sitting next to me, Sam on the bench across from us. Murph leaned in to kiss me whispering, "Hey beautiful, how are you today?" His eyes sparkled.

"Good," I looked around trying to think of a way to make Sam go away.

I didn't know where to start. I fidgeted as if I were trying to get comfortable. I stood up, sat back down, and started to say, "Listen."

Sam cut me off, "Murph, Tisha seems to be having trouble starting this conversation so allow me. I have some question I need to ask you."

Murph looked from me to Sam. "Ask, I have nothing to hide. I'm here to help."

"What's your connection to Brickyard Mike?

"Other than having shot him, nothing."

"Chester Adams."

"I don't know him." Murph's eyebrows rose and he looked to me for support. I lowered my eyes and stared at my feet.

"Can you tell me about the money that was recently wired into your bank account?" Sam's steely glare darted through Murph.

He got up and raised his hand pointing at Sam, "What are you implying? You're investigating me aren't you? What the hell are you wasting your time for? I'm a cop or was a cop. I'm one of the good guys and I'm on your side. This is bullshit." His eyes turned to me, "Tisha, you can't believe I'd be involved in any of this?"

"I don't. Really, I don't, but Sam made a few good points. If it were someone that didn't know you…" my voice trailed off. I couldn't face him.

"I can't believe you don't trust me. I threw everything away for you. I killed a man to protect you." He stomped away. I was not going to let him walk away angry. I caught up to him, grabbing his arm.

"Murph, please, let me explain."

He pushed my hand away, spinning to face me. "What do you think? That I have your brother? Or that I had Brickyard Mike slit your throat? What about our connection? What about your grandmother's house? Didn't that mean anything?" He searched my face looking for some acknowledgement.

"Of course it did. I want to get to know you better. I want you to be a part of my life, but I need to know. Where did you get that kind of money? It's between you and me. I promise. Just you and me."

"Okay. You and me. I make things. They're wire sculptures. I lived above a garage and used the garage as my studio. I started back in school. My family, being a family of cops, thought I might be gay because I was into art, so I've kept it a secret rather than suffer the constant ribbing, humiliation and intrusive questions. Their support is relegated to manly pursuits. These last few years as a cop and the bullshit that got me promoted made me realize I had to get out. It was one thing to be a beat cop and drive around all day looking for something to do, getting an occasional call about a car accident or a once in a blue moon a domestic, but getting promoted to detective and the homicide division wasn't in my plans. Looking at death isn't something I want to get used to. I switched to nights and during the day worked harder and harder and created a portfolio of sculptures. They're meant for outdoor display. They are big and not very portable, so I started networking with other artists and found some interest in outdoor gardens and buildings with green spaces. I put together a video and brochures and started marketing. I sold four pieces about eight maybe nine months ago, and another two last month. Last night, after I got home, I had a call on my machine; a garden in Philly wants to buy twelve pieces. The money and the exposure are huge. I've proved to myself that I could do it. It's my way out of the force."

"Oh Murph, why didn't you say anything?"

"I didn't find out about the Philly thing until late last night. Thought I tell you all about everything today."

"How did the hearing go?"

"I was cleared, but I handed in my resignation. I can't do this double life any more. I can't bear the thought of having no choice other than to use my gun. But most of all, I never want to stare into dead eyes again."

"I so understand. Are you okay?" I put my arm in his as we walked toward my apartment.

"Everything has been so overwhelming. First my draw to you, then the shooting and now my overnight success that took ten years of welding in secret. I need a breather." He gave me the smile that melted my heart.

"So what do you sculpt?"

"Fairies."

"I should have known." I knew I wasn't wrong about him.

"What does that mean?"

"I'll fill you in later. Listen, I did some brainstorming and created a board and did some online research. Want to come take a look?"

"Yeah, sure, but what about Sam?" He nodded his head toward where he stood.

"I'll talk to him. I think his bark is louder than his bite. There's something I'm missing, maybe a trained detective will see it."

"I'm only a detective for two more weeks. Sorry for blowing up. It's good that Sam is covering all his bases, even if he's 100% wrong. Has he gotten anywhere?"

"You seem to be suspect number one," I giggled.

"Great, why don't we all sit down and see what we can come up with. Maybe we have some real leads."

"Okay. Let me go talk to him. Head on upstairs, we'll be right behind you."

"Sounds good." I watched as he made his way to my apartment. What a butt.

CHAPTER 7

We all looked at my board, flipped through the stack of files I printed and took turns pacing around the house and coming up with theories. None of them made much sense.

"I think we need to get back to motive. Why would someone want Mario DeVito and me dead and what do they want with Bill and what does my uncle have to do with it?"

"Tisha, you need to break it down. Maybe they aren't all related. Maybe it's a coincidence with the killing on the train. There wasn't much in the way of press. As far as the police were concerned it was more than likely one thug killing another," Murph said.

My eyes widened, "So no one was looking for the killer?"

"After a body was found. But once we identified him, Mario's death was chalked up to an internal mobster feud. It was unofficially closed. If something comes to light, like a murder weapon then maybe it would be reactivated."

"What about when I told you I thought it might be Brickyard Mike?"

"I talked to Detective Nelson about it. He made it clear that unless we had a weapon and a live video of it happening or clear fingerprints on the gun, he was told to drop it, so he did."

"I don't understand. Murderers can go free?"

"Now you understand why I couldn't continue on the force. Nelson told me Brickyard Mike was a Fed informant. He was wanted for a slew of executions. It was hands off until the sting went down. Then he would be placed in witness protection. Brickyard knew if he went to prison he'd be killed, but he also knew if he put away a major figure, the mob would search him down and kill him. Your uncle was his ticket out. Chester Adams is low level on the fringes and will work with anyone to make some cash. I'm guessing Brickyard found out that you were on to him and he thought you would ruin it for him. Maybe he wanted to know what you knew."

"Why does everyone think I know anything? This is crazy. I sat away from all the action in my fishbowl cubicle. I couldn't hear anything if I tried."

Sam had been sitting back listening.

"Okay, let me continue with this train of thought from another angle. Brickyard knows he isn't the killer so he's not hiding from anyone. He is worried about the sting and getting fingered as a snitch. Kevin O'Sullivan did kill Mario DeVito. What is his connection to your uncle?" Sam asked.

"Never heard of him. Brickyard was the one who came to the office," I said.

"He's higher up on the food chain. He's a professional hit man. He'll work for anyone from the mob to the Russian syndicate and everyone in between. He's not a hothead like his brother. Had been arrested for some petty crimes, but that was when he was a kid. The DeVito killing excluded," Murph said rubbing his eyes.

"What do you think the DeVito killing was about?" Sam asked.

"That is still a mystery," Murph answered.

"Okay. From what I'm thinking, we dismiss Brickyard and DeVito for now. Let's focus on O'Sullivan and your uncle. What is the link between them?" Sam added.

"I need to do more digging. What about Beatrice?" I asked. A thought came to me. It was something Sven, I mean Ken Gallant, said to me right after we witnessed the DeVito murder. He said most crimes were about two things, money or a woman. I shared, "What if it was about a woman?"

"What?" Murph and Sam said in unison.

"What if O'Sullivan killed DeVito over or about a woman? Somehow my uncle is involved. Beatrice lived in Elmont, right next to Woodside. She was a waitress until a few months ago, not sure where, but it's unlikely she traveled far to get to a waitressing job. Somehow she met my father and married him in a flash. How would she know how to target him and how to land him in record time? My brother was always working on top-secret things and never shared. What if Beatrice and my uncle plotted together to get close to my father to spy on Bill so they could find out what he's working on and steal it or sell it?"

It was as if light bulbs flashed over both Murph and Sam's heads.

"Let's do some digging on that angle," Murph said. He looked down at his watch, "I have to go. My shifted starts in a few minutes. Let me see what I can come up with by asking around. How about we meet back here first thing in the morning?"

"Sounds good," Sam agreed. "Good thinking Tisha. Ever think of security work?" He smiled.

"Not really. Too scary, but I might be able to help with computer tracking. On a consultant basis."

He laughed. "Get some rest. I'll check on you later and see if my men have come up with anything." He walked out the door.

Murph took me in his arms; bringing his lips to mine he kissed me. I pushed him away, "If you start with that, I'm not going to let you leave. Go to work. Ten more shifts and then you're all mine."

He grinned, "You're a cruel woman. Out to the grind. I'll call you later. Be careful."

"I will. Watch your back," I said. I needed to do some serious digging.

CHAPTER 8

Typing away on my laptop, I searched for Elizabeth Allen. There had to be something I was missing.

Finding a closed Facebook account, I did my magic and voilà, up the old info popped. There were likes, stupid sayings, old YouTube videos and nothing useful. Scanning my brain, I tried a dozen more searches not getting anywhere. My head was pounding, a migraine on the horizon. Padding my defeated self to the bathroom, I searched the medicine cabinet for some Tylenol. I closed the mirror and jumped as a figure appeared behind me.

"What the fuck?" I screamed, "Get out of here. There's security everywhere." My mind scrambled trying to think of a way to get around this maniac and to safety. It was Brickyard Mike.

"I'm dead. I can't do none of that physical shit," he said looking at me like I had three heads, "You're the one that had me killed."

"No. This is nuts. What do you want?" I searched around the bathroom looking for something, a way to arm myself.

"I'm not going to hurt you. I'm going to help you."

Wary of this man I said, "Why don't we go into the other room." At least in the main area I had half a chance of running outside.

"Yeah, sure."

I made my way into the kitchen and found he was still with me. I didn't want this maniac here and needed to take control of the situation. Fiona taught me a way to summon spirits, but not how to get rid of them.

"Why are you here?"

"You got rocks in your ears? I said I was here to help. Don't look like you've gotten too far. And your brother is gone, right?" He was wearing the same dark clothes he wore the day he stabbed me. A bullet hole staining his shirt.

"Yes, my brother is missing. I prefer not to use gone unless you want to enlighten me. How can you help?"

"I was brought up a Catholic. Since I didn't get to do my penance, I figure if I help you out maybe St. Peter will look the other way when I get my interview."

"Okay." Was this guy for real? Well, not for real, he was dead.

"When I saw you on the train, I was trying to warn you. Your uncle, he's a good guy, but he's so greedy. There's enough to go around and when you have windfalls you need to parlay it, otherwise next thing you know you got your back against the wall and Vinny is staring you down ready to put a bullet between your eyes cause you can't even pay back the vig. But in your case it's Demitri."

"You're losing me, whose Vinny and Demitri?" I shook my head not understanding what he was saying. He seemed to be adding more people to a list of suspects growing to unmanageable proportions.

"It's an expression. Your uncle was playing both sides. He worked with the boys in Queens and Brooklyn with a sports and lending business. He was doing good. He had a nice place, a Benz and took trips to Miami, what? Three, four times a year. But it wasn't enough. I know he came from money. He complained about being cut off from the real cash for the past few months. He needed a big score so he did something stupid."

This scary hunk was making sense. "Go on."

"I'm getting there. I feel like a snitch, but better a confessing snitch in heaven than getting beat on in hell. So back to your uncle. He goes over to the other side. The Russians. Not the usual drugs or girls either. Tells them he can get access to some new weapon that's way worse than any WMD that Bush couldn't find. I told him I was out. If he didn't deliver, those crazy dudes would kill him and everyone associated with him. I went to the Feds. That morning I got shot; I wanted to warn you to stay away and not get caught up in the mess. I never saw a man hate his family as much as that man hated yours. It made no sense. Blood is blood where I come from."

"But you slit my throat," I shouted. He was as dumb as a brick wall.

"No, you smashed my foot and the knife got away from me. Then that yahoo preppy boy cop shot me."

"Why didn't you say you were trying to help me?" I searched his face; it showed years of hard life.

"Not my style. I couldn't be sure if anyone was watching and I was already a snitch once."

I shook my head and sat down; leaning back I tossed the Tylenol in my hand into my mouth and swallowed.

"So what did you want to tell me? Do you know where my brother is?"

"I told you about your uncle. The other part is sketchy. The Russians were going to take your brother to a warehouse and get him to replicate the device he created. As long as he cooperates, I'd guess they would want him alive."

"Where?" I pleaded.

"Let me think," he paced around the room. "The brother lives out on the Island, that would be your father. There was a warehouse we used to use in Glen Cove. There was an old dock across from it. Ferries went to the casinos in Connecticut, but it's been deserted for years. I'd put my money on that."

A sense of relief came over me. I had one more question.

"What about Beatrice. I mean Elizabeth Allen?"

"Betts? She's a piece of work. I told my brother to stay the hell away from her. The two had been on and off since high school. My cousin Mario mentioned something about what your uncle was planning. She did her research and found out your father was divorced, available and rich. When Kevin found out about it, Mario was dead meat. Kevin's a hot head. Told him he should've married her a long time ago. He's not the type to marry. He's one hard bastard. Has no problem killing people. I think he gets off on it."

The thought of a person "getting off" on killing people made me sick. Kevin O'Sullivan must be a sociopath. I didn't blame Beatrice for changing her identity and getting away from him.

"One more question." A knock on the door shattered the connection between us and Brickyard faded in an instant like a puff of smoke. Sighing, I got up and answered the door. It was my father.

"Dad, how are you?" His eyes told the story without having to have asked. The bags beneath them, the bloodshot tinge; all adding up to worry and lack of sleep.

"Not good." He held his arms out and I stepped in giving him a big hug.

"Sit down," I motioned for him to come into, "Coffee?"

"No. I can't eat, I can't sleep. I want Bill back," he fought back the tears.

"I do, too. I have a lead. I need you to stay here with me."

"What is it? Are you okay?" He sat up looking more worried.

"All this will be over soon. Trust me. I need to do a little digging and then we'll talk. Why don't you stretch out in the bedroom and try to take a nap?"

"Maybe I will. I am dead tired." He shuffled into the bedroom looking like he might collapse on his way.

Locking the front door, I went to my laptop and began typing. Scanning my memory for files in a file cabinet at work, and company names on the mail that came to the office, I remembered a few names and searched. After the third try, bingo. A warehouse in Glen Cove listed in the company name CJA Enterprises. Chester James Adams.

Texting to Sam and Murph as fast as I could, I wrote, *42 Garvies Point Road, Uncle Chet's warehouse, across from old Ferry, Russians involved.* I hit send.

Waiting for a response, I placed my phone in my pocket and made myself an espresso.   Looking at the clock it was almost midnight. Quitting time for Murph. A tap on the door startled me. I inched the curtain back, Sam appeared. Unlocking the door, I walked outside so we wouldn't wake my father who was snoring.

"Where did you get that info?" He placed his hands on his hips.

"I'll tell you later. What are you going to do?"

"I'm putting a team together. We downloaded the building plans and are meeting in fifteen to come up with a strategy."

"I want to help," I offered.

He smiled. "I don't think so princess. This is going to get dangerous if your brother is being held there and by the Russians. I contacted the Feds. They need warrants and it can take some time. I'm trying to pull in some favors and get it expedited."

"Wait a minute. You might not need a warrant," I said thinking, how could my uncle buy a warehouse with his disastrous financial record? I slipped back inside retrieving my laptop. Doing a records search, I came up with the information that I hoped for.

"CJA is an S Corporation with two shareholders. Chester James Adams and Kathryn Ann Adams are equal owners. We might not need a warrant."

The two of us flew down the stairs heading to my Grams' cottage. Pounding on the door, she opened it with a start.

"What is going on? Have they found Bill?" She was dressed, as always, in perfect attire. She did plug herself in.

"Grams, there isn't time to explain. Can we have your permission to search a warehouse in Glen Cove that you own with Uncle Chester?"

"What could be in it that you need to search? He was going to store furniture in it, but the roof leaked and it was quite musty. I don't have keys for it. Wait a minute. Do you think Bill is in it?" Her eyes widened and brows rose. "Of course you have my permission."

"Not sure if that's the place, but it's the best lead we have." I kissed her cheek, "We'll be back."

Sam was talking into his shoulder shouting, "We have a go. Meet at base now. Drop everything, now."

"What's happening?" The adrenaline was storming through my body.

"I'm getting my team together and we're going to plan our raid. The Feds will be joining, but with your grandmother's okay, I don't have to wait. I want you to go back to your place and stay there. Do not go anywhere until I come back for you. Understand?"

"Yes. My dad is with me. Be careful." He jumped into his truck and speed off.

The guard at my door gave me a smile and patted my shoulder as I went back upstairs. I wanted to be there but knew I would be in the way. My cellphone buzzed. Looking down at the face, it was Murph, *Talked to Sam, on my way over to help. Be over after. Stay safe.*

I texted back, *I hope this is it. Be careful.*

CHAPTER 9

I did as I was told and sat waiting. I paced, sat down, got up again, paced some more and then the proverbial light bulb went off in my head. The Ferry dock in Glen Cove across the street from my uncle's warehouse was undergoing a massive revitalization. Condos, storefronts and green space were all being constructed. With all of that activity, there had to be cameras. I started a search. After a few tries, I was able to piggyback in on the feeds.

Moving from camera to camera, I found one with a bird's eye view of the warehouse. The parking lot for the building was empty. A lone street light was the only illumination so I couldn't see any lights or activity in the old brick structure. All was quiet. Half an hour passed and still nothing. My eyelids were getting heavy. Fighting sleep, I made myself a cup of herbal tea, fearing the jolt any more caffeine would be to my system. As I brought the cup back to the table, I watched the feed show three large dark SUVs creeping up to the building. A few minutes lapsed and another four joined the trio.

Heavily armed men, I counted twenty-eight, wearing flak jackets alighted from their vehicles and in a well-orchestrated fashion converged on the building. From a peaceful nothingness to high powered commotion in a flash. Floodlights lit the exterior, burst of light shone from the few windows at the top of the long building, and after what felt an eternity but was a mere eight minutes, the double doors of the freight bay opened. Three men, hand on their heads, marched out followed by six flak-jacketed men. I held my breath praying Bill would appear.

Steps from behind me broke my concentration. Turning, I saw it was my father.

"Honey, I guess I did fall asleep. Are you okay? What are you doing?" Fear went through every pore in my body. I didn't want him to see this live feed if I was wrong and Bill wasn't in the warehouse. Or worse. What if Bill didn't make it? My need to know got the best of me. I couldn't pull my eyes away. My father would find out what happened one way or another.

"Dad, I received some information about where Bill might be held. Sam and his men as well as the authorities are raiding the warehouse right now. I'm watching a feed of surveillance. It's live."

His eyes bulged. "Move over." He sat down and the two of us were breathless waiting for some sign that Bill was there and he was safe. The three men that were led out were patted down, handcuffed and placed into police cruisers. The suspense was unnerving. I wanted to call someone and find out what was going on inside, but knew I would be hampering the task force's efforts. We stared at the screen, not wanting to take our eyes off of it for a minute.

My father broke the silence. "How did you find out about where Bill might be?"

"It's a long story," I answered wanting to tell him about my strange abilities and new other worldly guest.

"I'm not going anywhere." He looked at me the way he did when I was a child and did something wrong. He had already been privy to what I did, but wanted me to admit to the offense. Busted was the word that flew through my head.

"I don't know how ready you are to hear this, but here goes. You know about that weird ability I have to see people's thoughts if I touch their hand? Well it's morphed."

"Okay. Your mother had a similar ability. I think she could read minds. I guess you could call her a psychic. What has yours morphed into?" Crossing and uncrossing his legs, he began to rub his cheeks and eyes.

"Dad, sometimes dead people appear to me and talk." I said it watching his face for signs of comprehension.

"Can you give me an example? I'm having a hard time putting my head around this. Maybe if you tell me more, it would make sense." As our eyes met I could see the hurt when he mentioned my mother. It broke my heart.

"Earlier this evening, Brickyard Mike came to me. He wanted to explain why he was following me. He described it as his penance so when he meets St. Peter his sins would be absolved and he could get into heaven." Dad's eyes narrowed and he shook his head.

"Dad, I know it sounds crazy. They're not all like that. The others all need to resolve something before they pass to the next dimension. I'm not saying there is a heaven and hell or God or St. Peter or that I know any more than you do about what happens after we die. But, I do know that some people have unfinished business they need to fix before they can let go and move on. They come to me for help."

"Have you been able to help?" He smiled that proud smile I've so longed for.

"I think so. Brickyard Mike told me about a warehouse in Glen Cove. I did some digging and found a property that Grams owns with Uncle Chet. Sam and I went to Grams and she gave permission to search it. Otherwise we would have had to wait for a search warrant."

Still nothing from the scene. Men were milling about, but not another soul emerged from the building.

"Okay, but I still don't understand. Why do they want Bill?"

"It might have to do with a device he was developing. Somehow word about what he was working on leaked out and someone wanted access to it." My eyes widened as I saw some of the task force racing across the street and out of view. Going back to my original feeds, I highlighted another feed, splitting the screen and watching as a large boat descended upon the dock. Gunfire between the land crew and the boat began with flashes of light popping across the screen. I could see men on the land diving down for cover. A helicopter above shone its light on the vessel. A coast guard boat appeared; soldiers armed and ready. After a few tense minutes, the first boat was boarded by the coast guard, the riders apprehended, placed in cuffs and lined up on the dock.

I focused my attention back to the warehouse. Even though there were more than a dozen men involved in the operation, there was no mistaking Sam. He looked to his left and then his right. He turned his head back into the building and resumed his walk forward with a wobbly Bill trailing behind him.

"It's Bill, Dad. It's Bill!" I screamed.

"Oh, thank God, thank God." We jumped up and hugged between the tears of joy streaming down our faces.

CHAPTER 10

My father wanted to go back to his house, but I told him
Sam insisted he stay with me until he got back to us.
He wanted to call Beatrice and let her know where he
was, but I reminded him of the late hour; asking him to lie
down again. He agreed with little protest as long as I promised
to wake him when Sam arrived. Checking on him a few
minutes after he retired, I found him fast asleep.

Although Bill was found, my work wasn't over. There were
still two people out there who wanted to harm my family. Uncle
Chet and Kevin O'Sullivan were on the loose. They needed to
be caught and prosecuted for their crimes.

Typing away, I found little. They had no presence on the
web other than arrest records. I needed more firepower and
reasoned it was for a good cause. I hacked into major credit
card systems. Using various names I recalled from credit card
bills that came into the office, I scanned the transactions over the
past few weeks. One search stood out. A card with the name
Jimmy Chester revealed charges originating in New York. Most
were mundane purchases of groceries, drug store items and gas
highlighting the bill. Then a few weeks prior, the day I was
stabbed, charges started coming in from other states. New Jersey,
Delaware, North Carolina and Florida all had charges for gas
and food. The charges continued in Florida concentrating in
Marathon in the Keys. Although there was no charge for a hotel,
a new entry occurred daily for the Barracuda Grill.

I made copies of my findings, bundled it all into a zip file and sent it off to Sam. Uncle Chet was going to have to face the music; paying for what he did. He was wrong, very wrong about me. I was nothing like him. I didn't feed off of people and then run and hide when things didn't go as planned. My renewed faith in myself gave me a sense of pride. Pride that not only was I good at something, but when I put my mind to something; not only could I do it well, I could do it better than anyone. Oh yeah, Tisha was back and kicking ass.

CHAPTER 11

P icking my head up, I shook my head trying to remember why I was sleeping at the kitchen table. The cool marble was soothing against my face and although not the best way to sleep, I had been quite comfortable. The noise that roused me continued. Trying to get a focus on where I was and what I was doing was challenging given my lack of sleep and sapped energy from constant adrenaline rushes and mending a slashed throat over the past few weeks. It was the door. The damn door had more people knocking on it in the last couple of weeks than all of the time I lived in the city.

Plodding over to it, I pulled the curtain back to be greeted by Sam and Murph. I tried to open the door, banging my head on it when I pulled as the door was locked. Doing a retry, I unlatched the lock and moved aside to allow them entry. Before I had a chance to ask them what happened, I felt myself being lifted off my feet; a wet kiss slapped my cheek.

"Tisha you're the best sister ever!" Bill screamed.

I stood at attention. A smile spread across my face, tears of joy streamed down my face and then I slapped him upside his head as hard as I could.

"What the hell was that for?" His eyes bulged with surprise.

Sam stepped between us.

"Bill knows. We'll talk later. I'm so glad to have you back. Coffee?" I smiled making my way to the coffee machine.

The three erupted in chatter, trying to highlight their raid on the warehouse. It was difficult to decipher what each was saying. It was clear the raid was a success. My dad walked in, his hair shooting out in all directions, his face aglow and smiling. As he embraced Bill, there wasn't a dry eye in the room.

Sam mouthed to me, *call you later* and left.

Bill and my father headed for the door attempting to go to the main house.

"Wait, why don't you stay here?" I tried to figure a reason to give for them not to go home rather than explain that Beatrice or Elizabeth or whoever she was, might be involved.

My father looked at me, "Honey, we're okay now. It's over. Bill's home."

I looked to Bill and then to Murph, "Is it? Are we finished with this nonsense or is someone else going to be crawling through the cracks trying to screw with us?"

Murph started, "We rounded up the Russians who were holding Bill, our timing perfect because there was also a boat with some key figures aboard that had been eluding the Feds and a host of other law enforcement agencies for years. We think they were just about ready to move Bill. We got them all."

Bill interjected, "I don't think anyone else is involved other than the top guys who run these syndicates. They're not coming to New York or the States anytime soon."

"I'm talking about people closer to home," I said throwing a glance at my father trying to telepathically communicate the threat that may come from Beatrice.

Bill looked at me with the best *what?* look he could manage without saying the word.

"Do we know if Uncle Chet was involved?" I knew he was and would share. I wanted to see what they knew first.

"Yes, I'm afraid he is the one who set all of this in motion. Sam got an anonymous tip that he is in the Florida Keys. The

Feds are on their way to try and find him. It's a matter of time," Murph said.

"Anyone else?" Why didn't they understand I wanted to keep Dad away from Beatrice?

"That appears to be the group. Once they're questioned we should know more. At least one of them will flip," Murph said.

"I can't take this anymore. What about Beatrice? I'm sorry Dad, but she might have her hands in this. I don't want Bill to go back into the house only to find himself in the hands of the serpent." I looked from Bill to Dad. "And Dad too."

"Honey, I know all about Beatrice." Dad wrapped his arm around me. "I wasn't blind when I married her. I am my mother's son. I did a complete investigation on her. I know she changed her name and made up a persona. She *was* born in the south. Her father was in the military and her mother followed him to a base in Mississippi. When they split up, she and her mother returned to Queens. She had a rough life. It might have been a targeted meet up, but I do care for her and she for me."

"Why didn't you say anything?" My tension eased.

"What was I going to say? I didn't want to embarrass her. Little by little, she's been opening up. She hasn't given me her name yet. I know it's really Elizabeth Allen."

"I feel better. Go, I think we all need to sleep for a few days."

"Night princess. Sleep well. Oh, and to be on the safe side, the guards will be here a few more days," Dad said giving me a hug.

"Night. See you in the morning," Bill added, lightly jabbing me in the ribs.

Turning to Murph I gave him some wide-eyed appreciation. "I saw the whole thing on a live stream I set up. Tell me about it." We made our way to the sofa, he held me in his arms squeezing me closer to him. He turned and kissed me. The need to hear details of the night's event flew from my mind. It didn't matter. I was where I needed to be.

CHAPTER 12

The next week flew by, each day melding with the previous. There were police, Federal law enforcement and lawyers questioning my family trying to build a case against the men arrested. Free time was at a minimum. The bustle of the days was tiring because I was still recovering from the injuries I sustained. The whole mess was behind my family. I knew that soon, I would need to make decisions about myself.

Making my way down to the garage, I opened my art closet and began pulling out pieces of pottery, vases, mugs, mirrors, platters and flowerpots, placing them on a sturdy metal cart. I brought my wares into the garden, placing them between flowers or atop old stumps and photographed them. It's amazing how when you don't see something for a time, it becomes more beautiful. My pieces were unique. Some were stunning. All quite sellable.

Loading the cart back up, I returned everything to the closet. Heading upstairs to my space, I started the task of organizing the pictures. Next, I reregistered my domain name and went to work on a website. Finally, I figured out how Etsy works and opened a store with a dozen of my pieces. The excitement loomed inside of me anticipating the moment the site went live. Fireworks went off in my head as my efforts became cyberspace reality. Pimping my wares was next. Coming up with various enticements kept me busy for days.

Murph was relegated to a desk job for the remainder of his tenure as a detective. I hadn't seen him, he was also busy getting his collection together and ready for shipment down to Philadelphia the following week. Once I had my website up, I promised to help him create one. It's funny how when you aren't whining about money and lack of work and simply put your mind to doing what you love, it comes. I think a book has been written about it.

Bill had made himself scarce. He hid in his room or plunked away on his robots with the garage doors locked. He knew I was angry with him and I'm sure he knew why. Beatrice was planning a celebratory diner and invited Sam and his men as well as Murph to thank them for helping my family. It was tonight.

The day rushed along with me busy cataloging, marketing and creating a strategy for my site. Sam had e-mailed asking for some help on a case. He needed my expertise in finding some information and he was going to pay me more than I had seen in a long, long time. It would go far in paying my father back the money I owed him for bailing my life out. A few more jobs like that and some sales of my art, I could think about looking for a place back in the city or maybe Brooklyn.

Weeding through my closet, I picked out a deep blue wrap dress that flowed down to mid-calf. I added an Esmeralda Designs[2] deerskin necklace with blue basha beads, and completed the outfit with a pair of Vince peep toe booties with a three-inch heel. After a quick view in the mirror, satisfied with my choices, I applied mascara and a hint of blush. As I returned the makeup to the medicine cabinet, I heard a light knock on the door. Expecting to see Murph, I stood back when Bill appeared.

"Hey," he said.

---

[2] https://www.etsy.com/shop/esmeraldadesigns?ref=l2-shopheader-name

"Hey yourself," I answered.

He gave me one of his *I'm sorry* looks. It wasn't going to cut it.

"What do you want?" I crossed my arms not wanting him to plead his case.

"Don't be mad at me."

"How can I not? What is wrong with you? How much is enough?" I asked moving about, pretending to tidy up.

"I don't know what you're talking about or why you're angry with me. Please tell me."

"Bullshit. I'm not angry, I'm furious. How the hell could you put everyone through all of this?"

"What do you mean?"

"Stop with your poster boy for the next Noble Prize crap. WMDs? Seriously? How much were they paying you? Were you in on this whole mess, too? How much is enough with you? Look around, isn't all that we have and a great job to boot, enough for you?" Hands on my hips, I knew he couldn't skirt the question.

"I wasn't involved in the kidnapping," he answered, eyes lowered like a disobedient dog.

"Would you please stop with the dancing around. You were kidnaped because someone wanted the weapon you were creating. You were creating it. Doesn't matter who has it, who wanted it or who paid you for it. You made it and it was made to kill people. That in my book makes you a lowly, disgusting waste of my time. I should have let them keep you. How much did you sell out for?"

Slapping him couldn't have stung more than my words.

"I'm so sorry. I got caught up in a discovery I made that was happenstance. I told my bosses about it down in Pittsburgh.

They were paying me five million for the prototype and another five upon completion." His swallowed hard.

"Ten million to fuck up the world. Are you proud of yourself? You make me sick." I motioned for him to leave. As he opened the door, in walked Murph.

Looking from my brother to me, he said, "Am I interrupting something?"

"No, Bill was leaving." As Bill walked out, I slammed the door behind him.

"Come at a bad time?" Murph was walking on eggshells.

"No, perfect time. He and I have to get past a few things. Ready for the shindig? Beatrice had a cleaning company come in to combat the dander and relegated the feline clowder to the attic. I'll bring a Benadryl with me in case I start sneezing over her chitlins."

"Oh boy. This is going to be fun," Murph rolled his eyes.

"We'll talk about it later. I'll try to behave," I said reaching up to kiss him.

"We start this and we aren't going anywhere."

"Okay, but when I give you the escape sign, we're out of there."

"What's the sign?" Murph asked.

"You'll know." I smiled and led the way to the house.

Ringing the bell, I opened the door and called, "We're here." The sounds of laughter filled the hallway getting louder as we approached the formal dining room. Its mahogany table polished to a shine; placemats were set showcasing china and silver with crystal goblets finishing off the settings. The chandelier was muted with low white candles providing a beautiful glow to the room. The French doors were opened and the party was outside enjoying pre-dinner cocktails. Hugging my dad and Grams, I made my way around shaking hands and introducing Murph and myself to the security guards I hadn't met. I was civil to my brother yet kept a good distance between us.

As I finished my greeting rounds, a new arrival appeared. It was Fiona. I met her worried glance and went over to her. Giving her a big hug, I said, "I am so happy to see you. You belong here as part of the family."

"I wasn't going to come. I've been on edge ever since this whole mess started. The house looks beautiful and so do you." She hugged me and walked to my father. Their eyes met, Fiona held out her hand to shake his. He took one look at it and opened his arms. I could see a tear running down Fiona's face.

Beatrice walked onto the patio wearing a dress sporting an inordinate amount of ruffles. She announced dinner would be served soon and disappeared back into the kitchen. I chugged my drink down, the boozy concoction warming my cheeks, scooped another from the punch bowl and repeated the process.

"Slow down, Tisha. Don't spoil your dessert," Murph whispered in my ear.

I giggled, "Promises, promises." The booze loosened me up. Taking Murph's arm, we walked into the dining room and took seats as far away from Bill as possible.

My father watched as everyone took their seats. When all were comfortable, he tapped his glass and rose. "Thank you all for coming tonight. Beatrice and I would like to thank all of you for taking part in the rescue of Bill and the apprehension of his captors." As he spoke, servers went from guest to guest pouring champagne into flutes. He picked up a new glass. "A toast. Please allow me to quote Shakespeare: I can no other answer make, but thanks, and thanks."

There were some here, here's; a raising of the glasses and the conversation and food began. Course after course of interesting food was plated and presented with a new wine selection. Beatrice outdid herself. More like she found a fabulous caterer.

Murph seemed to be enjoying himself as much as I did. The gentleman next to me, Charlie, was a retired lieutenant colonel in the Army and quite a storyteller. He kept us in stitches with his funny tales with unexpected twists. Ready to give the go sign to Murph, I inched a little closer. A tap on the shoulder thwarted my attempt. Looking up, Beatrice was beside me.

"Yes," I glared not wanting her to intrude on my fun.

"We haven't spent any time together. Thought we'd catch up." She smiled at me in such a way it reminded me of the wolf dressed as grandma in *Little Red Riding Hood.*

"Betty, we don't have nothing to catch up on because we don't usually talk. All the same, why don't we keep it that way?" I mimicked her phony accent and with all the alcohol I consumed, was louder than I thought. The room was silenced. I looked around the table from face to face. Ruining the evening was not in my plans, but it was accomplished nonetheless. Embarrassed, I ran out and up to my place. Why did I let her get the best of me?

A knock on the door roused me from the pile I made of myself on the sofa. Dragging my butt to the door, I was happy to see Murph.

"I'm so sorry. I don't know what it is about her. She makes me see red." He pulled me into his arms.

"Some people are like that. You need to rise above it and minimize the effect she has on you."

He was right. "I'm a jerk." Nuzzling in his arms.

"No, we all had a little too much to drink and tongues can fly. Why don't I put you to bed and we can fix it all in the morning." He led me to the bedroom.

"But I thought you were staying?" I pleaded.

"You'll be asleep in a few minutes. I want your full attention." He lowered me onto the bed. He was right, before I could think another thought, I was asleep.

CHAPTER 13

R olling over, I spied that the clock read five thirty. A stream of light violated the curtains throwing its rays on my eyes rendering me unable to sleep. Curse the spring and its early daggers of light. Dragging myself out of bed, I made it to the bathroom, did my thing and then splashed a healthy dose of cold water on my face. Rather than go over my bad decisions of the previous night, I decided to move forward. Walking to the armoire, I pulled out a pair of leggings, a tee and a jacket. Anklets and sneakers on, I made my way outdoors for an early morning run.

I traveled the local streets, pushing myself to find my stride. I passed tree lined streets, early morning dog walkers and a few cars going their way, starting their day. Pushing all thoughts other than the moment out of my head, I savored the cool morning air, the sunlight that shone on my face and the way my body was responding to its first real exercise in what felt like months. I was alive and I had power.

Circling the streets and back home, I stretched and went back inside. Showering, I changed into jeans and a tee and headed out to the Smart car. Driving to Rocco's bakery in Glen Cove, I checked the clock on the dash, it read just after seven. The shop opened at seven. I ordered two batches of croissants and mini pastries asking for separate bags and got myself a cup of coffee. Back in the car, I headed to an all-night drug store. Picking out a card, I searched my purse for a pen. I wrote, *Beatrice, sorry for my outburst. The party was lovely. Had too much to drink.* I drove back home and pulled in front of the main house. Knocking on the door, I opened it and left my olive branch in the guise of pastries with a card on the kitchen table.

Tiptoeing out, I heard a voice behind me. It was Beatrice.

"Tisha?" she called.

I turned around; wanted to bolt, knowing it was time to face the music.

"Beatrice, listen, I'm sorry. I shouldn't have talked to you the way I did last night. It was wrong and I apologize. I left a peace offering on the table."

She smiled and said, "All I ever wanted was to find a good man, an honest man and have a family. I made some bad choices in my life and then some really bad choices. When I met your father it all changed. I changed. At first, yeah, maybe I was a fraud. That's not the case now. I adore him. I will do whatever it takes to make him happy." She was talking without her drawl. Her expression somber.

"I've made mistakes, too. We all do. It's just that, I know things. Things that people don't want to share, I know. Call it a gift, call it a curse, call it what you may; the fact remains. It's there and I can use it to help or I can hide it and a part of myself that makes me unique will be buried. Do you know what I'm talking about?"

She took a step closer. "Your father and I had a long, long conversation last night. He told me everything. And I told him everything, too. No more secrets."

"Okay. Are you ready?" I held out my hand to her.

She reached for my hand and I took it. She wasn't lying. She did love my father and her intentions were honorable.

"I still need to work on myself. I've got a plan. And you are right. We do need to catch up or better yet, why don't we try to get to know one another?" I asked.

"Nothing would make me happier." Beatrice smiled. "Want to join us for breakfast?"

"No, I'm off. I need to see a man about a fairy."

"A what?" Her eyes squinted reverting to her southern speak.

"Never mind. We'll catch up later. Maybe we'll do that girls' day out at the spa." I waved and headed out.

Back in the car, I plugged an address into the GPS and waited for the coordinates to spit back. Following the directions, I was hopeful. Hopeful that this beautiful man who did amazing things with my heart and whose hands melted my soul would feel the same way about me.

Pulling into his driveway, I could understand why Sam thought he was a suspect. Nary a blade of grass grew on the lawn, windows on the garage were blacked out and the stairway leading up to the second floor was shabby and broken. Careful to not fall through the steps to my death, I made it to the landing with my treats in tow. I knocked and waited. Butterflies were an understatement.

From the other side of the door, I could hear locks opening, and then with a flourish, the door swung open.

"Who are you?" I asked of the stranger who opened the door.

"Funny question. You're the one knocking on my door."

His eyes looked familiar, a bright blue. As did his height and smile.

"I was looking for Murph. Agamemnon Murphy."

"My brother. He doesn't live here. His shop is downstairs. He's over on Spruce."

As he closed the door, I called out, "What number?"

"Twenty-eight," he said as he closed the door.

Plugging in the new address, I made my way to Spruce Street. Parking on the street in front of his house I was pleased the home was well kept with his car parked in the driveway. I rang the bell and stepped back. Nothing. Rang again. Still nothing. I knocked. Realizing the art of surprise doesn't work unless the surprisee is at home; I got into my car and was about to head home. In the distance, I spied a jogger with a familiar gait. Turning off the ignition, I got out of the car and waited at the curb. A grin graced his handsome face as he approached.

"Hey, lady. How are we feeling?" he said joking.

"Fabulous. Met your brother." We walked toward the house.

"My brother? Which one?" He opened the screen door, took a key from his pocket and opened the front door.

"Not sure. The one that lives above your workshop."

"Atticus. He's a little rough around the edges. What were you doing there?"

"Looking for you. I thought you lived over the workshop."

"Used to, but then I found this place. I kept the other one for the workshop and when Atticus and his wife split, he took the apartment. Let me show you around."

We went through the small house. It was neat, freshly painted and in need of furnishings.

"Breakfast?" I asked holding up the bakery goodies.

"You bet, but first," he held me in his arms and kissed me. The rest, well I don't kiss and tell.

After a few hours, we got around to having breakfast. He ground the coffee beans while I rounded up plates, cups and napkins setting the table.

"I'm heading out to Philly in a few days to begin the installation of my art. I'll be gone for at least two weeks." His demeanor grew serious.

"Okay. We can talk on the phone," I said trailing off; wanting to scream, *take me with you.*

"Want to check out my work?"

"I can't wait." We finished our meal and got into Murph's car. We parked and walked to the garage doors. He pushed a few buttons and the doors sprang open. The nymphs and sprites that danced me through my childhood greeted me. At the center of all was Boon, the fairy who helped me understand my powers.

Smiling, I said, "Murph, you're not going anywhere without me. This is amazing. Where did you get the idea to make these fairies? A book or something?"

He shrugged his shoulders, "I don't know. A dream maybe."

"Well, let me introduce you to my childhood friends."

I went from sculpture to sculpture explaining their names and what they did. I knew with every ounce of my being ... I had finally made the connection of a lifetime.

AUTHOR BIO

Susan Peterson Wisnewski is an indie author from the Northeast. She writes thrillers filled with suspense and a sprinkling of chick lit and horror.

From a cruncher of numbers to a stringer of words, she decided it was time to follow her dreams and put down on paper all of those stories that floated around in her head. Raised in New York City and Long Island, she is a consummate shopaholic having been given the gift of style from her mother and grandmother. When not writing, she can be found shopping, visiting museums, gardening, or being walked by her oversized puppy.

Her books are a genre mix all neatly packaged together. Surprise and twists keep her readers guessing and she has been accused of writing books that can't be put down. Pushing characters to challenge themselves is her trademark as is a creating strong female characters – no damsels in distress here. Her inspiration comes from seeing a situation and then enhancing it to create an unusual story line. And yes, she does see ghosts, or spirits as they prefer to be called, and has had her run ins with a fairy or two.

OTHER BOOKS AND LINKS

Books don't create themselves. I have been fortunate enough to have several beautiful people help in the creation of this book. I'd like to give a special thanks to my sister Brenda for all of her help beta reading and pointing out inconsistencies. A super, special thank you to my editor Trisha who is more than amazing and was able to make my words sing. And to the blowtorch fairy herself, Christina, whose jewelry can be found sprinkled throughout this book and whose art can be found at: https://www.etsy.com/shop/esmeraldadesigns?ref=l2-shop-info-name.

Thanks wouldn't be complete without mentioning two online groups that have helped me move forward in seeing my dream through: the RWA crew and Wendy's Clubhouse.

Connect with me online at:
http://twitter.com/SPWWrites
http://facebook.com/SPWWrites
https://www.goodreads.com/SusanWis

Signup for my newsletter where you will find updates and giveaways on my website:

http://spwwrites.com

If you enjoyed reading *BlindSight*, I would appreciate if you would help spread the word about my book so that others can enjoy it too! Recommend it to friends and if you're so inclined review it on Amazon or on GoodReads. If you live on Long Island or in Southern Vermont and would like a guest author at your next book club meeting, contact me at susan@spwwrites.com.

Get ready for the next book in this series *InSight*, where Tisha learns more about her gift and uses it in her tumultuous life.